"Come on, Grady. The statute of limitations has long expired on breakup hard feelings."

"Says who?" He shoved an extra pillow behind his head. "From where I'm sitting, I'm still mad as hell." He downed his second longneck and went in for a third.

Jessie had the gall to cross her arms and roll her eyes.

"You think I still shouldn't be pissed? I asked you to marry me. You accepted."

"Almost a decade ago!" She smacked the dresser top. "Get over it. That's ancient history."

"The hell it is." He sprang from the bed, planting his hands on either side of her, pinning her in but not giving her the satisfaction of touching her. "Give me an honest reason and I'll let it go. More than anything, I want to let this—you—go, but you're stuck in my head."

"Sorry."

"I need a reason, Jess."

She raised her chin. "You know the reason."

"Oh, right—you don't love me."

"You know how much I care for you. You were my best friend. Why can't we just go back to that?"

"No, thanks." The friend card had long been off the table.

Dear Reader,

The SEAL's Miracle Baby may be set in the fictional town of Rock Bluff, Oklahoma, but in my heart, I imagined the poor people of Moore, Oklahoma, who lived through the all-too-real horror of having a large part of their town demolished by an F5 tornado.

At 2:56 p.m.on May 20, 2013, the tornado touched ground and devoured everything in its 1.3 mile-wide path for seventeen miles. Two schools were hit and many, many homes and businesses were lost. Twenty-four people were killed and 324 people were injured.

Especially heartbreaking was the fact that this is the fourth tornado to hit the city in fourteen years. In 1999, Moore was struck by its first F5 tornado. It killed thirty-six people and caused $1 billion in damage. (Thanks to livescience.com for these statistics.)

The entire state watched on live TV while these monsters roared. From afar, I remember feeling helpless. I can't even imagine what those poor people felt trapped in the heart of the storm.

In *The SEAL's Miracle Baby*, Jessie and Grady are both victims, but in different ways. When they're charged with caring for a mystery infant who miraculously survived the storm, they both face challenges they never expected to encounter. The biggest obstacle of all? Abandoning their hearts to love.

Happy reading,

Laura Marie

THE SEAL'S
MIRACLE BABY

LAURA MARIE ALTOM

HARLEQUIN® AMERICAN ROMANCE®

Recycling programs
for this product may
not exist in your area.

ISBN-13: 978-0-373-75571-4

The SEAL's Miracle Baby

Copyright © 2015 by Laura Marie Altom

Printed in U.S.A.

www.Harlequin.com

Laura Marie Altom is a bestselling and award-winning author who has penned nearly fifty books. After college (Go, Hogs!), Laura Marie did a brief stint as an interior designer before becoming a stay-at-home mom to boy-girl twins and a bonus son. Always an avid romance reader, she knew it was time to try her hand at writing when she found herself replotting the afternoon soaps.

When not immersed in her next story, Laura plays video games, tackles Mount Laundry and, of course, reads romance!

Laura loves hearing from readers at either PO Box 2074, Tulsa, OK 74101, or by email, balipalm@aol.com.

Love winning fun stuff? Check out lauramariealtom.com.

Books by Laura Marie Altom

Harlequin American Romance

The Buckhorn Ranch Series

The Bull Rider's Christmas Baby
The Rancher's Twin Troubles
A Cowgirl's Secret
A Baby in His Stocking

Operation: Family Series

A SEAL's Secret Baby
The SEAL's Stolen Child
The SEAL's Valentine
A Navy SEAL's Surprise Baby
The SEAL's Christmas Twins
The SEAL's Baby
The Cowboy SEAL

Visit the Author Profile page at Harlequin.com
for more titles.

This story is dedicated to the town of Moore, Oklahoma. May your skies be forevermore blue.

Chapter One

For all practical purposes, Rock Bluff, Oklahoma, was gone.

Navy SEAL Grady Matthews pulled his rental sedan onto the highway's shoulder, being careful not to hit a pink bathtub that rested on its side in a nest of debris. He lowered his window, bracing his forearm on the vehicle's frame to take in the tragic view. The early-May tornado had been damn near a mile wide, and it had razed everything in its seventeen-mile path.

When his dad called, asking him to help rebuild their ranch, Grady thought he'd exaggerated the degree of the storm's damage, but if anything, Ben's description had been inadequate. Grady's brain knew that a hundred yards down the road was where the historic Flamingo Motel should be, along with a McDonald's, an Arby's, the First Baptist Church and the Dairy Barn, but all of it was just gone, as if God had swept His hand over it, wiping the slate clean. Only the resulting mess wasn't clean. It was an unfathomable pile of concrete blocks and upended church pews and— Tears stung his eyes.

He wanted to blame those tears on dust from a passing National Guard convoy, but the truth was that all he seemed capable of focusing on was the fact that the last place he'd seen Jessie, held her hand, begged her to give him another chance, had been at the Dairy Barn. They'd sat in the back booth that always caught the afternoon sun. Her honey-gold hair had come alive in the glow, and he'd reverently skimmed the crown of her head, kissing the soft waves of her hair, inhaling the simple strawberry sweetness of her shampoo, because it hadn't been enough to just touch her—he'd needed to breathe her in.

I don't love you, she'd said. *This…us… We're just not going to happen.*

An hour later, Grady had signed his recruitment papers down at the strip mall that was now also gone.

He couldn't quite wrap his head around the fact that physical proof of his memories—the only thing left of him and Jessie—had been erased.

His cell rang. The caller ID read Rose Matthews.

"Hey, Mom."

"Hey, yourself, sweetie. Where are you? Almost to town?"

"Yeah, I'm just sort of taking it in."

"It's a shock. Your dad and I have had a few days to get used to…well, everything."

"Sure…"

"I do have some good news, which is why I'm calling. You remember Jessie's parents, don't you? Roger and Billy Sue?"

"Yes, ma'am…" He released a long, slow exhale.

"Well, they heard we've been staying at the shelter, and since they have that cute little guesthouse out by their pool, they asked if your dad and I would like to stay with them until our house is done."

Grady leaned his head back and groaned. Seriously?

"Since the guesthouse is just the one room and the bathroom, Billy Sue said she'll put you in one of their spare bedrooms."

And Jessie? Because he could tell all the way from his current vantage that her downtown apartment building had been another of the storm's victims. His pulse doubled just thinking her name.

"I'm not sure if you've heard, but your poor Jessie's place—"

Could this day get any worse? "She's not *mine*."

"You know what I mean. Anyway, she's staying with her parents, too, but the more the merrier, right? I know it'll be fun for you two kids to catch up."

JESSIE LONG RUBBED the aching small of her back.

She'd been out here for hours, sifting through the wreckage of her apartment in the hot sun. It'd rained that morning. The air was so thick with humidity and sediments from the debris that it felt hard to breathe. For the plastic tub filled with clothes and a few pictures, was this really worth it?

She knelt, tugging a taped-together plastic spoon from beneath bricks and dirt and the stainless-steel kitchen sink.

Standing, tears welling in her eyes, she held back a sob while cradling the spoon to her chest. Of all the things she could have found, this was the most precious.

The last time she'd seen Grady had been at the Dairy Barn.

They'd shared their favorite booth in the back, and though he'd ordered Frito chili pie for them to share, neither had taken a bite. As usual, he'd gotten a spoon for her and a fork for himself, but both utensils had remained unused.

After she'd broken up with him, she'd quietly cried against his chest, but he'd pushed her away, telling her that she didn't get to use him for anything anymore. He'd fished her favorite pink Sharpie from her purse—the one she used for doodling when she got bored in class—and drew a messy heart in the bowl of her spoon.

See this? he'd said, waving it in front of her face, then snapping it in half. *This is what you did to my heart. You just broke it. Like it doesn't mean a thing. But it does, Jess. I freakin' love you. I gave you a ring. I wanna get married and have a big family. You and me—we'll build a house out by the catfish pond, and every night at dusk, we'll sit on our front porch swing, watching the kids play while the sun goes down. What's the matter with you? Why can't you see everything as clear as me?*

Stop, she'd begged, scooting off the bench's smooth seat. *I see everything*, she'd said under her breath. *Mostly, that you and me and all of your big dreams are* never *coming true. I don't love you.*

To prove it, she'd walked away—but not before taking the pieces of that spoon as one last souvenir of what might've been.

THE FAMILY RANCH was worse off than Grady ever could have feared. Once again, tears stung his eyes as he absorbed the full weight of what his parents had lost.

The four-bedroom home he'd grown up in was now no longer a home, but a jumbled pile of drywall, four-by-four studs and the shredded remains of the china cabinet his mom had dusted every Saturday morning.

The barn he'd done chin-ups in to prepare for basic?

Gone. The chicken coop? Flattened. His dad's workshop? A graveyard of tractor parts and mangled sheet metal.

The wreckage went on and on. It was so bad that he couldn't really even take it all in.

Grady had seen a lot of horrible things overseas, but even the worst didn't compare to this. Where the hell did they even start in making this right?

Hands on his hips, he released a long, slow exhale.

Off on the horizon, he spied his dad's truck heading his way. When that storm hit, if Ben and Rose hadn't been in Norman at a doctor's appointment…

His stomach cramped just thinking about it.

And where were the horses?

Two chickens sat on the underbelly of an overturned car. He didn't recognize it as belonging to either of his parents. Who knew how far it'd traveled?

A deep sense of loss overwhelmed him. He'd come home to help rebuild, but how long would this take? His commanding officer had given him two weeks, and then he was due back on base in Virginia. Two weeks wouldn't even clear the drive, let alone erect a house.

His dad pulled up, stopping the truck in what used to be the front yard. When he climbed out, he didn't have to say a word to convey to Grady how low he was feeling. His shoulders were hunched and his expression grim as he stepped in for a hug. "Wish we were meeting under better circumstances."

"You and me both. Where's Mom?"

"With that girlfriend of hers who moved a few years back to Norman. Your momma… She needed to get away from all this."

"Yes, sir. I understand."

His dad patted his back. "Good to have you home, son. Real good."

Grady wished he felt good or bad, or really just anything at all besides numb.

AN HOUR LATER, once his dad left to pick up his mom, Grady bit the bullet by showing up at Jessie's parents'. It was gonna be awkward and awful, and he'd rather pitch a tent in the pasture, but that would only upset his mom, so he pasted on a smile and strode up the wide porch steps.

"Aren't you a tall drink of water." Jessie's mom, Billy Sue, sat in one of six white rockers.

Cotton, a miniature poodle who hated everyone but Billy Sue, yapped in her arms.

"Cotton, hush." Jessie's dad, Roger—one of two town dentists—extended his hand. "Thank you for your service to our country."

Grady smiled at Jessie's mom, but not knowing what to say to the man who was the father of the only woman he'd ever loved, he just stood there like a damned fool, nodding like a bobblehead SEAL doll.

"Come on in," Roger held open the screen door on the Southern-fried McMansion, with its two-story white columns and hanging ferns. How had this place remained as pristine as ever while his folks' house was a pile of rubble? "At the moment, I don't have all that much to do since my practice was blown halfway to Kansas."

"Sorry to hear that, sir."

He shrugged. "Way I see it, I've got my family and home, so I came out a-okay. It was about time to remodel anyway."

"Let me know if I can help. Once Mom and Dad's

insurance money comes in, I'll be out at the ranch, but until then, I don't mind lending a hand."

"All this excitement has stirred up my emotions, and…" As if he was choked up, the man's voice cracked. He placed his hand on Grady's shoulder the same way he had when lecturing him on having Jessie home by midnight after prom. "If you don't mind my saying, Billy Sue and I both thought you would have been a fine match for our baby girl."

"Ah, thank you, sir." What else could he say to that? *Gee, sir, I thought so, too, but your daughter had other plans?* His heart galloped like a runaway horse. Was Jessie here? Was she inside? Lounging by the pool? If so, what would he say? What would she say?

"Grady—" Billy Sue trailed after them "—we've got the upstairs guest room all ready for you, and just as soon as your parents get back, we'll barbecue some nice ribs, okay?"

"Thanks. Sounds great." The whole town had crumpled around them—including her husband's livelihood—and all she could think about was hosting a cookout? Where had she even bought the food? Swenson's Meat Market and the grocery store had been annihilated.

In the den, while Jessie's dad settled into his recliner to watch a golf tourney on TV, Billy Sue set down the dog, then paused in front of the back staircase, gesturing for him to follow. "Come on, I'll show you where everything is."

Even though he remembered the home's layout, he trailed her up the stairs. Cotton formed the tail end of the parade, yipping the whole way.

"Jessie's staying with us, too, you know? I'm sure she's real excited for you to be home. Although I know for a fact, Grady Matthews, that you've been back for visits long before now. Why haven't you stopped by?"

"Mom kept me busy." Was Billy Sue kidding? Didn't she have any idea what her daughter had put him through? And what was wrong with him that after the trials he'd faced in becoming a SEAL, Jessie still held the power to get him all tongue-tied and queasy—and she wasn't even there. He couldn't imagine how bad he'd feel once she actually showed up.

Billy Sue tsk-tsked. "I'm gonna have to get on to her for that. Shame on her for hogging you all for herself. Poor Jess would've loved to catch up."

Enough. He stopped midway down the hall. "Mrs. Long—Billy Sue—I don't mean to start trouble, but there's something I need to get off my chest. Ancient history, really, but I guess it needs to be said."

She spun her wedding band around on her ring finger. "After the week we've had around here, I'm not up for more bad news."

"It's more like *old* news." He shoved his hands into his pockets. "You do know your daughter broke up with me?"

Her eyes narrowed. "No. No, I don't believe that for a second. Jess still has your prom picture in her wallet. I thought you two naturally cooled down when you joined the Navy?"

"I didn't even enlist until—" What was the use in explaining? "Ma'am, it's the truth."

AFTER HER LONG DAY, there was nothing Jessie would have loved more than to jump in the pool, but as filthy as she was, she didn't figure her dad would appreciate her clouding his water. During the storm, her mom reported that debris had rained from the sky. So much had fallen that her dad had scooped the pool floor with an extrawide snow shovel. But that was okay. More than okay, considering how much the rest of the town had suffered. They were beyond blessed to still have their home.

So why did she feel so low?

Maybe because even though her apartment hadn't been anything special, it'd been hers, and now she had nothing to call her own. Not only was the second-grade classroom she'd been so proud to teach in gone, but the entirety of Rock Bluff Elementary School.

"There you are." Her mom stepped out the front door.

"Hey." Jessie pressed the autolock on her rental Ford and nodded to the black sedan parked in front of her. "Who's here?"

"Actually, there's a funny story that goes along with that car."

"Mom…" Jessie wasn't up for one of her mother's epic sagas. She loved her dearly, but the woman talked more than she breathed. "I need a shower and a nap, and—"

"You'll never guess who's inside our house right at this very second."

Jessie's chest tightened. One of her old high school friends had told her Grady was back to help his parents. She sent up a silent prayer that whomever her mom was talking about, it wasn't him. *Anyone* but him.

She was still shaky from the storm, being trapped in her building's basement until volunteer firemen had rescued her and a few neighbors. Thank goodness school had already been done for the day. The only thing worse than what she'd already been through would have been experiencing the tornado's fury with her students.

To see Grady now, with her looking a mess, she'd die of mortification.

"And, ladybug, you wouldn't believe what he just told me."

Jessie gulped. "He?"

No, no, no, this isn't happening.

"Since Ben and Rose are staying in the guesthouse, it only makes sense that with their Grady in town, he stays here with them. And why didn't you tell me you broke up with him? You cried for months. We didn't think you'd be able to leave for college."

"Please, stop exaggerating."

"I don't hear a denial." Billy Sue opened the back door of Jessie's car and took out the plastic laundry tub Jessie had filled with clothes. They were caked with drywall dust and mud, and her mom wrinkled her nose at the smell. "These jeans could get up and walk themselves."

"I know."

"Why didn't you just leave them? We could make a fun weekend out of driving to Fort Worth or Dallas to find you a whole new wardrobe."

This was all too much. The storm. Grady. Losing her apartment and school. "I don't want new clothes, I want mine—anything to remind me that four days ago, I woke up in my own bed, ate my own cereal, drove my own car, taught in my classroom. Now I don't have anything. It's all just gone. I feel like I'm living in the Twilight Zone, and I need a break."

"Honey…" Her mother slipped her arm around Jessie's shoulders. "Don't you see? Having Grady here will make everything better. You'll see."

"Oh, my God, Mom. No, it won't. If anything, having him around will only make an already awful situation unbearable."

"Sorry to hear that." Grady stood on the porch, glaring at her.

Chapter Two

"Jess…" It might sound sappy, but Grady had lost count of how many times he'd dreamed of this moment. Only, it was all wrong. For starters, Billy Sue wasn't supposed to be there. And in his rich fantasy life, Jessie would smile as opposed to staring him down as if he'd sprouted horns.

"Grady." Her cheeks were tearstained, white T-shirt dirt smudged and ponytail tangled, but even eight years since the last time he'd seen her, she was still the most beautiful woman in the world. And judging by her expression, she was also still not interested in anything he had to say.

"You two have fun catching up." Billy Sue made an odd clucking noise, then bustled around the side of the house with Jessie's clothes basket toward what Grady remembered was the laundry room door.

Now that they were alone, Grady should've had something intelligent to say. He didn't.

"You look good." She appraised him. "Healthy."

Wow. Talk about a less-than-stellar evaluation. "You, too."

"H-How long are you in town for?" She'd tugged a strand of hair from her ponytail and twirled it through her fingers. It was a nervous habit. One he'd watched a hundred times during University of Oklahoma football games.

"Two weeks."

"That's not long." She twirled faster.

"Nope." What could've only been thirty seconds stretched into a year.

"It's good seeing you, Grady." She hitched her thumb in the direction her mom had gone, then started to follow. "I need to help wash clothes."

When she was gone, the sun shone dimmer.

No one in his whole life had hurt him the way she had. How many times had he told himself he hated her? He'd planned all the snide or clever things he would say when their inevitable reunion finally rolled around. Yet there it went, already come and gone, and he felt like a sixth grader ogling a high school cheerleader. What was it about her that had him trapped for all this time in her spell? How could he once and for all vanquish her from not only his mind, but his heart?

"GRADY LOOKS GOOD, doesn't he?" Billy Sue sprayed a pretreatment solution on Jessie's favorite jeans.

"He's all right." Jessie filled the utility sink with warm water, dumping in a few capfuls of detergent for her hand washables. She was so bone-deep tired that she was sure the gravity of what the next two weeks truly meant hadn't fully sunk in.

Other than her parents, the only person she'd ever loved was Grady. What did she do with that fact?

"Still have feelings for him?" Her mother shook matted leaves from a pair of sweats and into a trash bin.

"No."

"That why you broke things off?" Why did her mom keep pushing? It wasn't like her to be all up in Jessie's private business.

"If you don't mind—" she gave a pair of socks an extrahard shake "—I'd rather not talk about it."

"Honey…" Billy Sue blasted her with a look of parental concern. "Maybe I can help. All those years ago, I thought he left you for the Navy."

"He did."

"But you told him to go?"

Jessie shrugged. "I guess. Sort of. But, Mom, you know about…my situation."

"Wait—that's why you broke things off with him? Honey, why? Did you tell him and he was upset?"

Fighting the knot at the back of her throat, Jessie shook her head.

"He wasn't upset?"

"I didn't tell him."

"BILLY SUE, I CAN'T thank you enough for this meal and—" Grady's throat tightened when his mother's voice cracked "—your hospitality. I'm not sure what we'd do without you and Roger."

"Aw, it's our pleasure." Billy Sue and his mom shared a hug.

The early spring air held a chill, but the outdoor fireplace kept the area around the table warm. Jessie's parents' home had been built on the town's only hill, which meant the pool deck's view was expansive. On a clear night, you could just make out the Oklahoma City skyline. On this night, the National Guard's generator-powered emergency lights securing downtown Rock

Bluff punched through the dust just far enough to make it look like swirling ground fog.

Roger asked, "Grady, could you please pass the rolls?"

"Ah, sure…" He could, but that would entail looking at Jessie. Didn't her father know how hard Grady had worked to keep his gaze focused on anything but her?

During the exchange, their fingers brushed.

Jessie released the basket so fast that it dropped. Cloverleaf rolls scattered.

Cotton darted from beneath the table to sink his teeth into one, dragging it under an azalea bush.

"Sorry," Jessie said.

"No problem." Grady snatched the empty basket, setting it back on the table.

"It's a problem for me," Roger said with a chuckle. "I really wanted another roll."

For his mom's sake, Grady suffered through another thirty minutes of small talk, but then he helped clear the table and made a beeline for his room, where he'd stashed the six-pack he'd picked up from the lone surviving liquor store. It'd been a madhouse, and Grady couldn't say he blamed folks for wanting to drown their sorrows in a bottle.

He'd managed a whole five minutes of nursing a beer while studying the manual on the new dive computer he'd soon be using when someone knocked on his door.

"Come in," he hollered.

Only after Jessie entered, closing the door behind her, did he get the bright idea that he should've faked sleeping. A fact that shamed him back to grade school. The guys on his SEAL team would laugh their asses off to see how pathetic just a few hours spent around her had made him. Hell, on base, the guys called him Sheikh, on account of him having a virtual harem of women trying to get his ring on their fingers. What his friends didn't know was that Grady hadn't wanted any of them.

Jessie was his only girl.

He downed the rest of his beer and opened another.

"We need to talk."

"I'm sleeping."

"Don't be stupid." She hefted herself up to sit on the low, sturdy oak dresser. Not a good thing, considering she wore a denim miniskirt and tank top. When she crossed her legs, he caught a peek of yellow panties.

He took another drink, then covered his fly with his binder.

"All right." She tucked her long, distractingly gorgeous blond hair behind her ears. "So this whole setup pretty much sucks for both of us, but let's cut the tension and get through it like adults."

"How?" *Especially when that tank's hugging your curves like paint and I remember you riding me with that hair of yours hanging all loose and wild?*

"Come on, Grady. The statute of limitations has long expired on breakup hard feelings."

"Says who?" He shoved an extra pillow behind his head. "From where I'm sitting, I'm still mad as hell." He downed his second longneck and went in for a third.

She had the gall to cross her arms and roll her eyes.

"You think I shouldn't still be pissed? I asked you to marry me. You accepted."

"Almost a decade ago!" She smacked the dresser top. "Get over it. That's ancient history."

"The hell it is." He sprang from the bed, planting his hands on either side of her, pinning her in, but not touching her—not giving her the satisfaction of him touching her. "Give me an honest reason, and I'll let it go. More than anything, I want to let this—*you*—go, but you're stuck in my head."

"Sorry."

"I need a reason, Jess."

She raised her chin. "You know the reason."

"Oh, right—you don't love me."

"Of course not. It's been forever since I've even seen you. You're a stranger. I'm happy without you."

"Which is why your eyes are dilated and you can't stop licking your lips?"

"I need ChapStick."

"What was up with the leg crossing? You must've flashed me those pretty yellow panties a half-dozen times."

"Oh, my God, since when did you become such a perv?"

"What's perverted about me being a trained observer?" His gaze zeroed in on the erratic pulse in her throat. He tipped his beer to her. "Consider it a sign that your tax dollars are hard at work."

"You know what I mean…" Her eyes pooled with tears as she pulled in a deep breath.

"Damn straight, I do. But tell me, Jess, if you're so happy, why aren't you married with four kids, so no one has to ride alone on roller coasters? Isn't that what you always wanted? What *we* wanted?"

Her expression hardened. "Don't go there."

"Why not?"

"You're an ass."

He shrugged.

Yes, he was. But she'd hurt him so damned bad. Up until joining the Navy, all he'd ever wanted was to buy his own ranch, marry Jessie and start their family. He'd never sought wealth or glory—she was *all* he'd ever wanted. And that fact killed him. Hell, he'd been back in town less than twenty-four hours and already he felt crazy. It was downright embarrassing.

"What do you want from me?" she asked.

Everything. But mostly, the truth. "All I want is for you to finally be straight with me. Why did you break things off? I get it if you thought we were too young, or you fell for someone else, or I just didn't *do it* for you in the sack, but this is a small town. Folks talk. My own mother has told me you've never been serious with another guy."

"Just like you've never been serious with another girl?"

"Exactly. I'm the logical sort. Every day I deal with black-and-white facts. Look at us—we have jobs, all our teeth. Why haven't we moved on? Haven't you ever asked yourself that question?"

She looked away. "No."

Sighing, he took a step back, holding up his hands in surrender. "Fine. If that's how you want to play it."

"Grady…"

"What?"

"You know how much I care for you. You were my best friend. Why can't we just go back to that?"

"No, thanks." The friend card had long been off the table. Didn't she remember all those lazy summer days down by the creek? He'd kissed every inch of her, and it wasn't just his ego telling him she'd liked it. "For the sake of our parents, I'll be polite, but you can't go back in time and erase what we shared. I've been with other women since, and it wasn't the same."

She paled. "Gee, thanks. Good to know you've slept around."

"Can you honestly tell me you haven't?"

Again, she avoided his gaze. "You don't have to make it sound so dirty, but yes. I—I've had a few other *committed relationships* that turned physical—if that's what you mean."

"And…" He urged her to get to the heart of the matter. Had she shared a fraction of the chemistry with those other guys as she had with him? Obviously not, or she'd be with one of them now. "True love?"

"I'm not even dignifying that with an answer."

"In other words, business as usual?"

"What's wrong with you?" Eyes narrowed, she drew in her lower lip. "You never used to be this cruel."

"I'm not cruel, Jess, but direct. There's a difference."

"Semantics…"

"So, in summary, you want me to buck up and play nice?"

"Would that be so hard?"

More like impossible.

He rubbed his jaw, searching for the right thing to say when all he wanted was for her to tell him the truth. That day in the Dairy Barn that no longer existed, there'd been so much more to their story. There still was. Only, for whatever reason, she'd refused to end it. Oh—she'd verbally ended it. But in his heart—where it mattered— he couldn't help but feel as though they still had a long way to go before he, at least, found closure.

Chapter Three

"I know this is tough, everyone." The next morning, Jessie's school principal looked strangely out of character in his plaid shorts, Rock Bluff Elementary T-shirt, ball cap and sneakers. "But again, I need you to sift through this rubble for anything salvageable. Our budget is nil, so every pencil and pair of scissors counts. I fear most textbooks will be water damaged, but maybe a few made it out all right. Questions?"

When no one seemed unclear as to their mission, they got to work.

For safety reasons, no students were invited to help, but many faculty members and parents who lived out of the storm's path and whose homes were unaffected had come out to lend a hand.

Though the work was hot and messy and mostly unproductive, it did get Jessie away from her depressing apartment wreckage and her parents' house—or, more to the point, away from Grady.

Some of the things he'd said had been horrible. The only reason she hadn't lashed out at him had been the knowledge that her lies had created his animosity. Meaning she essentially had no one to blame for his derision but herself.

She remembered every second of their time together. Above all, she cherished the moments after they'd made love, when he'd held her warm and secure in his arms. They'd talked for hours about their shared future. Neither had had college aspirations. They'd both wanted to lead simple, happy country lives like those of their parents.

She knelt to pick up the tin-can pencil holder one of her favorite students had made for her. Paul was now in fifth grade. It made her heart ache to think the only children she'd ever have were her students, but that was okay. At least she was lucky enough to have a career she loved, where every day other people shared their smart, cute and funny kids with her.

"Your mom said I'd find you here." Grady stood near what used to be her students' cozy reading nook. He wore desert-camo cargo pants, heavy work boots and a blue Navy T-shirt that made his chest look broad enough to need its own zip code. She instantly yearned to touch him, which only made her resent his presence more.

"This is where I work," she snapped, "or at least it used to be. I can't argue with you."

"Who said I wanted to argue?"

"Then, why are you here?"

He shrugged, then shoved one hand into his pocket and took a sip from a jumbo drink from Ron's Hamburgers. It was strange how the storm had played God—selecting who got to keep their lives and who had to start over. Maude Clayborn—the owner of the burger joint—had drawn the lucky straw. Knowing Grady like she did, Jessie suspected he was drinking sweet tea. "Partially, I'm here because my mom made me. Mostly, because I owe you an apology for last night."

No, no, no, her heart cried. *Don't you dare be nice to me. Hating you is much easier than the alternative.*

"You're right, I was an ass, but you have to admit to leaving me in the lurch. You even kept my damned ring. That thing cost three summers' lawn-mowing money. Do you even still have it? Or did you pawn it?"

The very idea incensed her. "Of course I have it— somewhere." *I wear it on a chain every day to remind me to never settle for anything less than real love.* It was on now, dangling between her breasts.

"Great. Then, I want it back."

"You can't be serious. And anyway, the ring might be lost."

He laughed—only the sound struck her as more dangerous than jovial. "Oh—I'm as serious as getting an STD on your birthday."

Her eyes widened in horror. "Did you? You know, get one of those…on your—"

"Good Lord, Jess, it's just an expression."

She nodded. Of course. But with him being a Navy SEAL and better looking than any man had a right to be, she didn't doubt him having a girl in every port.

"And don't try changing the topic. If my ring's lost— find it. Since you don't want me, maybe I'll give it to some other woman."

Over my dead body. "Okay, but obviously I don't have it with me now."

"Fine. Just don't forget." He surveyed the mess, then sipped from his drink. "What do you need me to do?"

Leave! Unfortunately, if she wanted to finish this task by Christmas, she needed his help. "There's a pile of plastic sacks over there on my file cabinet. Grab one and start picking up anything of value."

GRADY WOULD BE damned if he'd let anyone at that school work harder than him. By the end of the day, he'd filled dozens of sacks with pencils and crayons and heart-breaking little school pics with scribbled notes on the backs.

The work was hot and dirty and he felt as though dust had settled into every pore.

Jessie's shoulders sagged, and the ponytail that had earlier that day shone in the sun now hung limp and coated in the same gray dust covering their bodies and clothes.

If she were still his girl, once they got home he'd have carried her to their shower, then scrubbed her down till her skin shone pink. Then he'd run her a bath, squirting in a healthy amount of the strawberry bubbles she'd always loved. Next, he'd have settled in alongside her, kissing her till the sun went down and the water turned cold. He'd fix her a simple dinner. Maybe steaks on the grill. He'd rub her aching feet and make love to her before they spooned into sleep.

They'd have the best night, every night.

But all of that was just a dream. And even though he could have kept on working for another twelve hours, he knew she couldn't, so he said, "How about we head back to your folks'? See what our moms cooked for dinner?"

She arched her head back, in the process showing him the mesmerizing curve of her neck. "Sounds like a plan."

On their way to drop off the last of their day's finds in the principal's truck bed, she said, "Thank you."

"You bet."

"Considering we're sharing the hall bathroom now, how about you shower first since you filled the most bags?"

"No way. I appreciate the offer, but ladies first. You look like hell."

"You're such a charmer."

"I try."

She cast him a go-to-hell glare. "Not hard enough."

BACK AT HER parents' house, standing beneath the shower's warm stream, Jessie closed her eyes, wishing it wasn't Grady's gorgeous profile her mind's eye chose to see.

While sudsing her arms and legs and breasts, it was his hands she imagined stroking her. His ring dangled, teasing her with thoughts of what might've been.

Because thinking about him hurt, she hurried to finish scrubbing the last of the day's grime from her hair, already dreading the task of doing the same thing all over again tomorrow.

Finished, she wrapped her hair turban-style with a towel, cinched her robe tight at the waist, then knocked on Grady's bedroom door to tell him it was his turn in the bathroom.

His door wasn't all the way latched, and it creaked open.

Nothing could've prepared her for the sight of him lying flat on the bed—naked, dirt smudged, but 100 percent glorious manly muscle. Though the proper thing to do would be to close his door, then dress herself for dinner; instead, she indulged in a long visual feast. He wasn't body-builder bulked up, but his broad shoulders had definition. His biceps looked far too big for her to fit her hand around, and his six-pack abs and lower, well...

She closed his door, granting him privacy while she ducked into her own room.

Stretched across her bed, cheeks superheated, she remembered all too clearly the times they'd skinny-dipped in the creek, when he'd held her on hot summer days in the cool, clear water. She'd wrapped her legs around him and together, they'd discovered just how well their bodies fit together.

The first couple times had been awkward—lots of giggling and fumbling with condoms. After they'd gotten the hang of it, she'd tired of having anything between them. Unknown to him or her mom, she'd made an appointment with a Norman doctor to get on the pill. It was there she'd described how painful her monthly cycles had always been. When the medicine the doctor prescribed didn't even dull her cramps, Dr. Laramie suggested Jessie undergo a laparoscopic exploratory procedure to check for potential causes of the pain. When Jessie's mom wanted to know why she hadn't told her about seeing a doctor, Jessie hadn't exactly lied—she just hadn't told the entire truth. When the doctor prescribed birth control pills as a way to regulate her periods and control pain, her mother hadn't given it a second thought—or, if she had, she hadn't mentioned it to her daughter.

When the diagnosis of endometriosis had finally come, and along with it, a speech on how she would most likely never conceive considering the severity of her condition, at first, Jessie hadn't believed it. Then, when her mom had broached the topic one day at lunch, sharing her concerns, encouraging her to go on with her life and talking about how many alternatives there were to natural pregnancies, only then did it start to sink in that the doctor's words had consequences.

In hindsight, she probably should've told Grady, but honestly? She couldn't have handled his rejection had he said the wrong thing. She hadn't been mature enough. She wasn't sure she was now—not that it mattered, since she still had no intention of ever telling him the true reason she'd broken their engagement.

She couldn't speak for his parents, but her own had been relieved when what they'd called her high school fling had cooled down. They'd dreamed of her completing college—not her dream, theirs. She'd been the dutiful daughter, and in the end had never regretted earning her degree. What had she regretted? Not being able to share her graduation with Grady. Or the high of getting her first job. Her first apartment. Her first legal beer. So many, many firsts that had been happy enough, but not nearly complete without him.

Since he'd gone, she'd felt as if her life had been lived with the sun filtered. And that had been hard, but by no means insurmountable. Way worse tragedies had been survived. Just like Rock Bluff would rebuild after the tornado, so would she.

Jessie blow-dried her hair, and when she heard the shower turn on wished her mind wasn't flooded with images of Grady's ripped, naked body.

She took extra care with her hair and makeup and instead of putting on yoga pants and a T-shirt, she chose a yellow sundress and sandals. Even though Grady had demanded she return his ring, it still hung safely hidden, where it would stay until she was good and ready to take it off. Maybe that day would come, maybe it wouldn't. Who knew what the future held?

All she did know was that for now, that ring had become a symbol of the dreams she still had for her life, and a promise to never settle for anything less than the magic she and Grady had once shared.

GRADY LOOKED UP from his poolside lounge chair and had to remind himself to close his mouth. "You cleaned up all right."

"There you go again with that charm." Instead of smiling for him, Jessie scowled. He couldn't say he blamed her. Out of all the things he could've said, why had that come out?

"Yeah, well…" He downed his beer, thankful he'd grabbed another couple of six-packs on his way home from Jessie's school. "I meant that you look good."

Billy Sue and his mom had set the table, but neither of the women or their husbands had joined them outside yet. Candles and tiki torches had been lit, and the sunset was a spectacular tribute to the power of life moving on.

If it hadn't been for the ocean of devastation spread before them, he might've envisioned they were on a date at a swanky seaside hotel.

"Feel good about what we found today?" The question was as lame as everything else he'd done around her lately, but at least it wasn't in any way confrontational.

She nodded. "I'd hoped to find more books without water damage, but considering how much rain fell not just during the storm but since, it's a miracle any survived."

"Sorry." He hated seeing her sad.

"It's okay. I mean, it's not, but…"

"I get it." The situation was what it was. In time, the town would be rebuilt, Jessie's classroom reimagined in a new location. The loss was overwhelming, but thankfully, very few lives had been lost—most on the highway where travelers hadn't had time to seek shelter.

"Wonder where everyone is?"

"Am I not company enough?" He'd meant his question to be light, but somewhere his joking tone got lost in translation.

Her smile was slow, but once she'd fully abandoned herself to the gesture, he was lost. The setting sun transformed her golden hair into a halo and he stilled just to drink her in. Warm, brown eyes and a slight build that'd felt so damned good against him. He could've held her forever—had always thought he would. But for them, forever hadn't lasted. And now, in two weeks' time, he would leave again.

Gazing upon her now, he selfishly wished he'd been away on a mission when his parents' call for help had come. Because he'd been far better off with Jessie out of his life. Now he feared never wanting to let her go— but the craziest part about that was she'd never really been his.

AFTER DINNER, JESSIE hightailed it to her room.

The guys were engrossed in an old Clint Eastwood Western, and her mother and Rose were playing cards.

Once again being seated alongside Grady for dinner had been painful. He'd smelled so good—of manly soap and a delicious citrus aftershave. Instead of eating her mother's lasagna, she'd wanted to gobble him.

When someone knocked on her door, her pulse raced.

Her mother poked her head through the door, sending Jessie's spirits into a downward spiral. "Ladybug, I know you've had a busy day, so I hate doing this, but I need you to drive into Norman."

"Norman?" Even without traffic, it was a good twenty-minute trip. Weaving through all the cordoned-off roads and debris piles would make it thirty to forty minutes. "Why?"

Her mom clutched her chest. "I'm having awful heartburn, and the only thing that'll help is that special almond milk I like, but you know the only place to get it is at that fancy health food store. Oh—and take my car. With all the debris, I want you to have four-wheel drive."

"Mom…is that store even open? And you know I don't like driving after dark. I have TUMS. Let me grab you some, and I promise to run to the store first thing in the morning."

Still clutching her chest, Billy Sue winced. "Oh—I called, and the store's open till ten. Plus, I already thought about your poor night vision. Grady's driving. He sees perfectly at night—well, he'd pretty much have to with all of that covert, black-op activity he's involved in. *Very* exciting, huh?"

Grady ambled down the hall in their direction. "Just grabbing my wallet, Mrs. Long, then I'm good to go."

"Mom!" Jessie whispered under her breath while Grady was in his room. "You don't have heartburn. This is some wacky setup attempt to get me and Grady to spend time together, isn't it?"

Billy Sue gasped. "Jessie Anne, that's insulting. Why would I manipulate my own daughter?"

Oh, Jessie could think of any number of reasons, but recognized the futility of bringing them up now.

Back to clutching her chest, Billy Sue cried, "The pain's so bad. Ladybug, you have to go. You know how hard my almond milk is to find. Grady's going to need your help."

Jessie rolled her eyes. "All right, Mom, calm down. We're going."

When Grady emerged from his room, Billy Sue miraculously recovered long enough to fish her car keys and a twenty from her bra. "Here, take these!" She jingled the keys and money at him.

The sound was Cotton's signal that it was time for a car ride, and he danced at Billy Sue's feet.

"Mom!" Beyond mortified, Jessie snatched the bulging OU key ring—not the money—then wiped it off on her dress. "Gross!"

Her mother clutched her chest. "The pain! It's so bad!"

Jessie took Grady by his arm, dragging him from the nuthouse formerly known as her childhood home.

Outside, she said, "Sorry about this. I'm ninety-nine percent sure this is a misguided matchmaking attempt, but there is that sliver of possibility that Mom's really sick."

"How about the fact that you have trouble driving after dark? Another *fib?*"

She wrinkled her nose, then held out the keys. "Unfortunately, no. Are you okay to drive Mom's SUV?"

"Sure—although for the record, I've driven smaller tanks." He took the keys, pressed the keyless remote, then opened her door. "And don't sweat the whole matchmaking thing. I had the same thought when my mom told me the *dire nature* of the situation."

"What tipped you off?"

"The fact that the whole time your mom stood in the middle of the family room, moaning and clutching her chest, your father's only reaction was to turn up the TV. Cotton didn't even wake up until Billy Sue headed upstairs."

"I really am sorry." Jessie climbed in alongside him. She'd ridden beside her mother a hundred times, but with Grady behind the wheel, everything changed. The vehicle usually seemed roomy—but his mere presence, and their past, loomed between them as if a third person sat in the middle.

"Don't be."

"Why not? Now that I think about it, I'm more than a little miffed that Mom would pull a stunt like this."

"Seriously—" he backed out of the driveway, then hit the neighborhood road "—don't sweat it." He lowered his window.

She welcomed the breeze. Fresh air had never hurt a situation.

"Let's just get this over with."

Now Jessie needed an antacid. Grady's clipped tone alerted her to the fact that for him, there was no statute of limitations on hurt feelings. She'd hoped to at least pass the time with small talk, but it looked as though the only thing small in this car was Grady's capacity for forgiveness.

Chapter Four

Grady was none too happy to find himself alone with Jessie. Even if the SUV her mom used for the day care smelled like a cross between Cheerios and crayons, Jessie's faint strawberry lotion wreathed him in familiar scent. The fact that after all these years he still remembered that sort of detail about her only made his heart ache more.

Trying to play it cool, as if being next to her wasn't killing him—he focused on driving along the five-mile stretch of blacktop country lane.

"How do you—"

"I take it—"

When they both talked at the same time, they laughed. For that instant, laughter was a good icebreaker, and loosened the knot between his shoulders. But then he remembered who he was dealing with—the woman who'd broken his heart. The returning tension hit like a two-by-four.

"You go first." Jessie angled on her seat. "What were you about to say?"

"Judging by the car, and the Toddler Time logo on the doors, your mom still runs her day care?"

"Yep. Can you believe she's also mayor?"

"Mom told me. How did that even happen?" As long as he'd been alive, the Rock Bluff political climate had been more of an old boys' club. "Don't get me wrong, I'm happy for her, but was surprised."

"Oh—I know. She ran on a lark. Her gardening club got bees in their bonnets about the old mayor—remember Fred Holscomb?"

"Sure. He'd been in office for, what? Like fifteen years?"

"Yep. Well, Mom's club went before the city council with a proposal to beautify downtown—you know, adding things like hanging baskets of petunias to light posts and parking a few ornamental trees in fancy planters."

"Sounds doable."

"That's what her club thought—especially since they'd raised the funding to make it happen. So they're at the meeting, and all the ladies brought in cookies and brownies and Opal Mayville's famous lemon bars for the council, when Fred starts spouting about what a pain his wife's front porch flowers are, and how he gets sick of watering, and how, come August, everything's just gonna burn up and die in the heat, so why even bother trying to plant anything? If it were up to him, the world would be a much better place covered in nice, low-maintenance concrete."

"He really said that right in front of your mom?" Turning onto Old Barnsdale Road, Grady winced at the thought of the female wrath that opinion had no doubt raised.

"Yes, he did. Well, the meetings are televised on the new public-access channel a couple of high school kids put together, and the way Mom laid into him was epic. When he tossed out the challenge that if she thought she could do a better job as mayor, he'd darn well like seeing her try, she took him up on his offer and never looked back. Last November, after the garden club and quilting club and just about every other women's group you can think of adopted her campaign, then voted in record numbers, she won in a landslide."

"Damn…" On the main highway, Grady dodged debris piles. "Good for her. How's she doing?"

"She's holding her own." Jessie's tone held a note of pride. "For the first time since Carter was president, Rock Bluff has a balanced budget, and the firemen and police are thrilled with the change, because they never run out of baked goods for their break rooms."

"Nice." In the heart of the storm's devastation, National Guard floodlights lit the way for dozer operators to work through the night. "So how does she have time for matchmaking and running her town and business?"

Jessie laughed. "Great question."

They passed through the worst-hit area in somber silence. It went unsaid that the downtown that Billy Sue had wanted to beautify was no longer there.

Even this late at night I-35 traffic crawled, as it had been closed on both sides down to just one lane. Overturned cars had been moved onto the shoulders, and looked as if a giant had been playing Matchbox and thrown a tantrum. The headlights sparked on bits of tempered windshield glass littering the road.

"I still can't believe this happened," Jessie said. "In my dreams, everything's back to normal, but then I wake and this nightmare is real."

"Might take a while, but things'll get better."

"I know."

His heart shattered when a glance her way showed

her eyes shining with unshed tears. A fierce longing shot through him. He wanted to hold her, to promise everything would eventually be okay. He wanted to skim her soft hair back from her forehead, then kiss her lips and nose and cheeks, comforting her, reassuring her, loving her the way he used to when she'd bombed a test or gotten a flat tire. Never had he been more keenly aware of the fact that the old saying about not knowing what you've got until it's gone was true.

They may have passed through the storm damage and now rode on a debris-free interstate heading north to Norman, but the personal wreckage between them spanned not miles, but time—nearly a decade. But no matter how much he wished to turn back those years, the Navy had hardened him, taught him to stay focused on reality. The here and now. And the reality of their whole, sad saga was that it was over.

His mind understood that fact.

The pain crushing his chest did not.

Away from her, it had been all too easy to compartmentalize what they'd once shared, to shove it into a dark corner, never seen by the light of day. Now, sitting her next to her, every so often catching whiffs of her strawberry lotion, made pretending she lived on a different planet kind of hard.

"Is being a SEAL everything it's hyped up to be?" she asked. "Are you always trudging through swamps, carrying tons of equipment on your head?"

"Sometimes." He tightened his grip on the steering wheel, glad for the opportunity to think about anything but his still-fierce attraction to her. "Depends on the mission. There was this one time when my team was hunting down a not-so-nice guy in a not-so-nice place I'm not allowed to mention when me and my friend Cooper drew the short straw and got stuck doing surveillance from a river. We breathed through snorkels and were only above water from our eyes up. We must've knelt on that muddy bottom for five or six hours when a snake passed by that was as big around as my thigh. Coop and I just froze. Like Indiana Jones, I can handle just about anything but snakes. Man, my heart beat so hard, it wouldn't have surprised me had the bad guys heard it up in their camp."

Jessie blanched. "That's awful. Remember the time that cottonmouth chased us out of your dad's catfish pond?"

"Yeah. Thanks for reminding me." Grady shuddered. "I especially recall the part where you jumped on my back and let me do all the running."

Her sly, sideways grin did funny things to his stomach. "Sorry, but you have tougher skin than me. Plus, you had on jeans and I was only in cut-offs and a bikini top."

His recollection of that particular view made him instantly hard.

Mouth dry, body wanting what he could never again have, Grady returned his attention to driving instead of remembering how they'd laughingly retreated to his old tree house, where he'd untied her top, and helped her out of her shorts.

As if she remembered, too, she turned from him to stare out her window. "That mean old snake's probably still there."

"Probably." *Along with the remains of what we once shared.*

"Sometimes I'd really love to shake my mother..." By the time Grady parked the SUV in front of the health food store that had closed two hours earlier, Jessie's nerves were shattered. She'd tried keeping conversation casual, but every topic led to times they'd spent together. "I knew this would happen, and I feel like a fool for not just calling myself to check the store hours."

"Yeah."

Yeah? Did that mean he agreed with her that she should have called? Nice. Too bad he hadn't always been this much of a charmer, or she never would have fallen for him.

They left Norman's quiet streets to rejoin the interstate's ever-present bustle.

Despite being surrounded by so many people in all the passing cars, Jessie couldn't remember a time when she'd felt more alone. Grady was right there—close enough that if she wanted to, she could reach out and touch him, skimming his strong, tan forearm. Or entwine their fingers. The knowledge that she would never again experience that sweet, simple pleasure of holding his hand ruined her. The pain collected at the back of her throat, closing off her air and stinging her eyes.

When her cell rang with her mother's familiar cheery tone, Jessie was so flustered by the weight of her and Grady's shared past that she struggled to even find her phone. "Hello?"

"I need you to do another favor for me."

"Mom…"

"No, this time it's serious." By the time her mother finished relaying the situation, guilt consumed Jessie for thinking she held the world record for heartache.

After disconnecting, she cradled the phone to her chest.

"Let me guess," Grady said. "She needs us to run another errand?"

"Yes, but you're not going to believe this... We need to drop by the Rock Bluff police station to pick up a baby."

"Wait—a *baby*?"

"You heard right. Crazy, huh? I guess the poor little thing was found in a field by the highway. It's a miracle she's even alive."

"Why'd they call your mom?"

"Because of the day care. She's a registered foster parent, and occasionally takes temporary custody of really young kids who are in rough situations—she even has a nursery set up at the house. Police told her they expect to run through the few license plates in the immediate area where the infant was found, and will most likely find her family within hours. Mom needs us to get the baby, because we have the car seat."

"Ah..." He took the Rock Bluff exit. "Makes sense."

Jessie alternately dreaded and anticipated claiming the infant for even a short while. Though she'd long since come to terms with her own childless situation, that didn't make it easier to bear when parents of her second graders brought baby brothers or sisters to Open House or parent/teacher conference nights.

In under ten minutes, Grady parked the vehicle in the chaotic police station lot. A makeshift volunteer camp had been set up in the adjoining empty field, and a tent city flattened the formerly tall grass.

Jessie didn't wait for Grady to open her door as she once would have. Even if urgency hadn't propelled her forward at a frenetic pace, they were no longer on terms where she'd have expected—or even wanted—him to pour on any level of courtesy or charm.

The station's lobby was even more of a mob scene than the parking area, but she spotted their mutual friend Allen, who had married her good friend Cornelia—aka Corny, Corn Dog or Corn Nut—and headed his way.

Jessie sensed Grady behind her, and walked faster through the crowd in a failed attempt to make the humming awareness stop.

"Holy shit," Allen said upon catching sight of his old football buddy. They gave each other slapping bro hugs. "Wish you were here under better circumstances, but it's good seeing you, man."

"Likewise."

"I didn't figure we'd see the whites of your eyes till Thanksgiving."

"I hadn't planned on being here," Grady said. "But once Mom and Dad told me about the ranch, I had to come."

"I understand."

While the men caught up, it was clear to Jessie that they regularly stayed in touch. That hurt. How could Cornelia have kept that information from her? Had Grady been to their house? Sat on the same sofa as her? Jessie's mind should be focused on the task at hand, but that was hard, considering her current level of betrayal. Who else in town had hung out with Grady and wasn't talking?

"I imagine you're here about the baby," Allen said, leading them out of the lobby's bustle to the break room. "Crazy to think that out of all this wreckage, this little sweetheart survived without a scratch."

The guys had made a corner nest for her out of faded,

neatly folded quilts that the local churches had donated to the jail.

"Oh, my gosh…" Jessie's heart nearly broke. "She's so tiny."

The blond-haired, blue-eyed cherub couldn't have been over two months old, and mud crusted her fuzzy pink PJs. Someone had been thoughtful enough to wash her face and hands, but her curls still held dirt and grass.

Jessie scooped the sleeping infant into her arms, cradling her against her chest. "The girl's parents must be frantic."

"I know, right?" Allen shook his head. "The thing is, out of all the missing persons' files we're working, none of them involve an infant. The chief's guessing her folks must have been among those injured on the highway, and that they were taken to an outlying area hospital. We'll run her DNA to have matched against the deceased in the morning. If you and your mom don't mind caring for her until we find them, it'd sure ease our minds, knowing this little lady's in good care."

"Of course," Jessie said, smoothing the infant's matted curls. "We'll be happy to keep her for as long as it takes you to find her true home."

AFTER BUCKLING THE baby into the safety seat, Grady climbed behind the SUV's wheel. Jessie rode in back, alongside their tiny new passenger.

Watching Jessie dote on the infant did crazy things to his insides. All at once, he was furious and sad and filled with resentment. How dare she deny him his own long-held dreams of becoming a dad? Of course, the moment that thought hit his head, he knew it was crazy, but sometimes that was exactly how he felt. Had he and

Jessie married out of high school, like Allen and Cornelia, they'd already have school-aged kids. The notion incensed him—just how fast his life was passing by. On the surface, he was happy enough. But peel back his carefully shrouded emotional layers and he was a freaking disaster. Which was why, aside from holidays, he avoided Rock Bluff and all of its inhabitants, who reminded him of what he'd lost.

Back at the house, the women fussed and cooed, bathing the infant and dressing her in fresh-smelling, soft pink clothes. A pediatrician friend of Billy Sue's stopped by, and pronounced the baby to be in remarkably good condition. Through it all, the exhausted tiny creature slept, blissfully unaware of how frightened she might be upon waking to find herself surrounded by strangers.

Grady wanted to join in the spectacle of adoring this miracle, but he'd been shut out. Not deliberately, but the fact that they assumed he knew nothing about babies, coupled with the sad truth that Jessie hadn't even made eye contact with him since they'd returned to her parents', told him loud and clear where he stood—on the outside, forever looking in.

Tired of lurking in the hall, hovering in the shadows just outside the nursery, Grady made his way downstairs to join his father and Roger in watching an old John Wayne war movie.

"How's it going up there?" his dad asked during a commercial.

"Good," Grady said. "They've got things under control." Which was a damn sight more than he could say for himself. The sight of Jessie holding a stranger's baby had triggered something in him that his knotted stomach refused to let go of.

His dad noted, "Your mom and I sure were hoping to get a grandkid or two out of you by now."

"Before this whole mess with the twister," Roger piped in, "Billy Sue and I were just talking about that same thing. We're not getting any younger."

"I could use a beer," Grady said. "You guys want one, too?"

"You bet." Roger shifted on his recliner. "And if you don't mind, bring my pretzels from the pantry—and that horseradish cheese dip Billy Sue hides on the lower shelf of the fridge. Look way in the back."

"Will do." Grady was relieved his stab at changing the subject had been a success.

Rummaging in someone else's pantry and refrigerator struck him as just about as uncomfortable as the whole grandkid speech. Come to think of it, since he'd stepped foot back in town, not a lot had been comfortable—except for those fleeting moments of shared laughter between him and Jessie in her mother's car.

From upstairs he could hear the faint sound of infant whimpers, and then a full-on wail.

Cotton added excited yipping to the mix.

Arms full, Grady returned to the family room.

"On second thought—" Roger aimed his remote at the TV to notch up the volume to cover the baby's cries "—Ben, maybe the last things we need are grandkids."

"Maybe so," his dad said, while, on the TV, John Wayne drew his gun.

With both older men engrossed in the movie, Grady took his beer and meandered out to the shadowy pool deck.

More power had been restored to the outlying areas

affected by the storm, but the swath of greatest destruction was still dark.

The screen door creaked open and then banged shut.

Grady looked over to witness Jessie dart from the house.

In the low light, she couldn't see him watching her as she retreated to a bench-seat covered swing. When she then started crying, Grady found himself in the unfamiliar territory of being unsure what to do. Since the day he'd earned his SEAL Trident, it had been drilled into him to make swift, fact-based decisions, but nowhere in any drill or manual had a situation like this been covered. Since Jessie had broken things off with him, his experience with women had resided solely in the realm of the temporary. Things were fun while they lasted, but the moment he was called out on his next mission, he cut things off with clinical precision. There were no hurt feelings, because he'd been clear from the start that whatever was shared was purely physical.

He might be brave in gunfire, but when it came to surrendering his heart? Forget it. Jessie had assured he would *never* love again.

Lord, he wanted to go to her, drawing her into his arms—not just to stop her tears, but figure out the reason behind them. But what good would that do? They were no longer friends any more than they were lovers. They were nothing. Strangers who'd happened to meet under difficult circumstances.

In stealth mode, using the shadows to his advantage, he crept from her line of sight.

But before retreating around the backside of the house, he made the mistake of taking one last look at her defeated form.

She sat sideways on the swing and hugged her knees to her chest. Moonlight shone in her teary eyes. The effort it took to stop from running to her damn near killed him. But for his own self-preservation—hell, self-respect—he had to avoid her like poison. Because to him, to his ego, to his carefully walled-off emotions, that was exactly what she was.

Chapter Five

Jessie raised the hem of the old high school softball T-shirt she'd changed into to dry her eyes. Crying about not having a baby wasn't going to get her one, and those extra few tears shed over what might've been with Grady were just plain wrong. He wasn't even worth her tears. He was a cocky cowboy-turned-SEAL who never would have settled for a broken mess like her.

She forced a deep breath and pulled herself together.

Before Grady's arrival, she'd never been prone to crying jags—although, to be fair, she also hadn't dealt with her entire town and life being blown to smithereens.

A coyote's lonesome howl summed up her feelings.

"I hear ya, bud."

Back in the house, the TV erupted with a WWII battle. From upstairs came the baby's now frantic cries.

Jessie wandered into the laundry room for peace, only to encounter Grady sneaking through the back door.

She jumped. "Jeez! I didn't even know you were outside."

He shrugged. "Didn't know I needed your permission to leave the house." Then he winced. "Is it always this loud around here?"

"Yes, on the TV. No, on the baby. Wanna go grab a

beer?" Jessie didn't know why she'd asked the question. But standing close in the confined space, she realized that after all these years her racing heart still recognized the scent of his breath, and she'd go anywhere with him if for no other reason than to escape the current chaos.

"I'm down. Only, since I'm already on my second, think you could drive?"

"Deal. I'll be right back."

She grabbed her wristlet wallet and keys, then dashed upstairs for a quick change into hip-hugging faded jeans, a white tank and cowboy boots. After yanking out her ponytail to finger-comb her long hair into messy waves, she added lip gloss, then rejoined Grady in the laundry room so the two of them could slip out before their parents had even noticed they were missing.

Twenty minutes later, they occupied two stools at the bar of the Dew Drop Tavern over in Schilling—also unaffected by the storm. The few times Jessie had been there on dates, it hadn't been this crowded, but then there had also been a dozen other establishments for folks to gather that no longer existed.

After their on-tap Buds had been delivered, along with a basket of hand-cut fries to share, Grady said, "Last time I was in this place was after that homecoming game our sophomore year when it rained the whole damn night. Allen and I thought we had it won, then lost in, what? Like the last ten seconds?"

"Technically, there had been three seconds left on the clock."

He winced. "Thanks for reminding me. Pretty sure my back still hurts from that game."

"So this is where you guys went, huh?" Jessie grinned, running her index finger around her glass's rim. "Corny and I waited for you two losers thirty minutes outside the locker room. When you never showed, we went to the dance alone and pissed. Come to think of it, your whole flat-tire story was pretty dumb, considering you could have just walked to the gym from the field."

"Sorry. Allen and I needed a guys' night, so we snuck out of the locker room through the coach's door."

"Creep!" She pummeled his chest, never meaning her actions as anything other than playful fun. But when Grady trapped her hands squarely over his heart, she discovered it beat as fast as her own. Suddenly he leaned in for what she hoped, thought, prayed would be a kiss, and she thought her heart would stop altogether.

And then he abruptly backed away to down the remainder of his beer before signaling the bartender for another.

For the second, maybe even third, time that night, Jessie's eyes welled, but she'd be damned if she'd give him the satisfaction of knowing she still cared. She didn't. It had been a good long while since she'd been kissed, and that craving—no, more like yearning—tugged at her heartstrings. Nothing more. If he were to dare claim otherwise, she'd slap his no-good, whisker-stubbled cheek for sass.

But he not only didn't make claims, sassy or otherwise, but wouldn't even look her way until after she'd eaten all the fries and he'd finished his third beer.

Mortification and loneliness didn't begin to cover the way she felt all crammed in next to him in the crowd, with their thighs, hips and shoulders brushing, and that achingly familiar attraction she held for him humming, when he seemed oblivious to her. In fact, when he went so far as to ask an old classmate of theirs—who'd wedged in on his other side in her too-tight jeans and a rodeo buckle practically bigger than her pile of fake red hair—to dance, Jessie threw up a little in her mouth.

After the twosome left, she might have gained breathing room, but she'd lost her ever-loving sanity.

The dimly lit joint was humming with energy as the whole place sang along to Toby Keith's "Red Solo Cup." The air was thick from smoke and far too many tall tales.

"Hey, little lady." A cowboy sporting a brown leather hat and obligatory Wranglers held out his hand and smiled. "Wanna *proceed to party*?"

"Sure." *Why not?*

It wasn't as if she had any reason to stick around the bar. She only carried her wristlet wallet, into which she'd stashed her keyless remote, credit card, cash and lip gloss—not that she'd even had need for the latter, since her first coat of the night was sadly in place even after munching all those fries.

She took the cowboy's hand, letting him guide her through the crowd to the dance floor, where she spied Grady and his redhead. He held his hands low on her hips, and had hooked his thumbs over the top edge of her leather belt. The girl from high school, whose name Jessie couldn't even remember, had tucked her hands into Grady's back pockets.

"What's your name?" the stranger asked.

Jessie told him, and they somehow made small talk over blaring, old-school Johnny Cash.

At the end of the song, her stomach sank when she realized that Grady was no longer on the dance floor. Had he taken the redhead outside for *air*? The very thought of him kissing another woman turned her stomach almost as much as thinking of herself lip-locking with another man did—ridiculous, in light of the fact that unless she intended to die alone, one day she would kiss another man and like it!

But not tonight...

"Thank you," she said to Bobby, a nice guy whose only fault was that he wasn't Grady. "This has been fun."

"Who says it has to end?"

She laughed. Great question. And so she danced with him again to a slow Garth Brooks tune about heartache and pain. Grady appeared through the shadows, as if the song had summoned him, and he asked Jessie's current partner if he minded if he cut in.

The pass-off was amicable enough.

The way her pulse raced like a caged hummingbird's was not.

"What're you doing, Grady?"

"Seems obvious, Jess." His breath smelled familiar and sexy and laced with just enough beer that she credited Budweiser for any sweet-talking rather than him. "I saw the prettiest girl in the room and claimed her."

"Oh, you did?"

"Hell, yeah..." He leaned his head low, nuzzling her neck, downright stealing what little strength remained in her knees. "And now I'm gonna kiss her."

"And just how do you figure on doing that when she wants nothing to do with you?"

"She might *say* that." He backed away just far enough for her to catch his sloppy wink. Sadly, this wasn't him talking, but too much beer. "But deep down, there's no hiding the fact that we share unfinished business."

"Oh?" She gulped.

He skimmed her hair back behind her ears, then framed her face, brushing her full lower lip with the pads of his thumbs. "See, I know a secret. She happens to love makin' out on dance floors."

Lord help her, but from the jukebox Brad Paisley and Carrie Underwood launched into "Remind Me," and Jessie was reminded of just how good it had once felt being held in Grady's arms. As for the possibility of him kissing her? The thought turned her all hot and achy and wanting. And she hated it almost as much as she craved even more from him. But being held by him was the emotional equivalent of letting a flame lick too close and then burn. No matter how beautiful and seductive Grady's flame was, she couldn't risk being burned again.

"Y-you don't know anything," she somehow managed, nudging him a safe distance from her. "And anyway, it's late, and I have to be back at school in the morning."

"Anyone ever tell you you're a buzzkill?"

Mainly just herself.

GRADY HAD A tough time opening his eyes the next morning.

Complicating the issue was the fact that not only had he made a drunken pass at the woman he'd sworn to steer clear of, but she now stood at the head of his bed, hands on her hips, scowling. "Get up."

He groaned, giving himself a leisurely scratch as opposed to leaping to attention like Miss Bossy Pants would have no doubt preferred. He could deny it all he wanted, but last night at that bar, they'd shared a moment—until she'd gone and dumped the verbal equivalent of ice water on his head.

"I mean it."

"What's the problem, and why the hell are you in my room?"

"Technically, it's my parents' guest room, and trust me, this is the last place I want to be."

He'd just now gotten around to noticing the background soundtrack of the wailing mystery baby and winced. "Your mom still hasn't found her folks?"

"No, and I'm due at what used to be my school in five minutes. In what I'm sure is another stupid matchmaking scheme, apparently you and I have been left to play parents all day, but I'm not falling for it." She charged from his room and presumably into the nursery just as the crying stopped.

After using the heels of his hands to give his eyes a good rub, Grady rolled out of bed, only to cup his throbbing forehead. How many beers had he had? All he remembered was wanting Jessie more than he'd wanted his first pickup truck, and then her shooting him down, and then the night pretty much turning south—*way* south, as in straight to hell—from there.

He groaned and wandered into the bathroom to relieve himself, then cautiously made his way to the nursery.

The baby had switched into high gear, and her supersonic wails no doubt had dogs barking clear to the next county.

Cotton was doing a bang-up job.

"Hush," he said to the yippy dog, plucking him up, only to gently set him out in the hall before closing the nursery door.

"Give me that baby."

"Why?" Jessie snapped. "You couldn't take any better care of her than Cotton could."

"If that's what you believe, then how come you woke me in the first place?" He crossed his arms.

"I don't know..." She jiggled and rocked and cooed, but the little lady wasn't having it.

What Jessie didn't know was that Grady held not just one ace, but a good half dozen up his sleeve. "Give me that kid."

This time, he wasn't taking no for an answer.

Just like he'd been taught over years of pulling baby-sitting duty for his friends and their wives back in Virginia, he first swaddled the infant nice and snug in a receiving blanket, then held her extraclose, tucking the downy-soft crown of her head beneath his chin. "There you go," he crooned. "I know you're scared, but we're gonna find your momma and daddy real soon."

He paced the length of the room nice and slow, and when her cries settled into whimpers, and then tiny huffs, and finally peaceful breathing, he couldn't help but feel a small rush of victory. Hot damn. He still had his touch.

Jessie's gaze narrowed.

Hands on her hips, she asked, "Where in the world did you learn how to do all that?"

He shrugged. "Must've picked it up from watching a movie."

"Uh-huh. Tell me the truth."

"For a few years, I was low man on the totem, which meant whenever the older guys on the team opted for a night out on the town with their wives, me and my pals, Wiley, Rowdy and Marsh, always seemed to get pulled for babysitting duty. Well, shoot, after a while, we started making a competition out of it—you know, see-ing which one of us the kids liked best. Marsh was the clear winner—especially once he had his own kid. Rowdy was a disaster, but we gave him points for trying. Wiley was so-so, but I did all right. My specialty was the babies. Maybe because they didn't realize I was faking it."

"What you just pulled off wasn't faking it, Grady, but a God-given skill. You were the same way with horses. Chickens, on the other hand…" She winced.

He laughed—but not loud enough to wake the baby who slept in his arms. "I still have a scar on my calf from where Mom's old Rhode Island Red nailed me."

"Could you blame her? I'd have pecked you, too, if you'd tried snatching my chick."

"How was I supposed to know which one was hers? We had about sixteen that year, and I needed the extra credit for science."

Now Jessie was laughing. "Who could forget the great chicken maze? I'm shocked NASA didn't recruit you for that one."

He rolled his eyes. "You're just jealous because it beat your mushroom collection."

"Whatever."

Lord, he'd missed this. Just the sheer, simple pleasure of their banter. Didn't she miss it, too? What was wrong with her that she couldn't see how perfect they were for each other in every single way? What was wrong with him that since being home, he'd thought of nothing else? "Why wouldn't you let me kiss you last night?"

"Wh-what?" She coughed.

"You heard me."

"I'm not sure what you mean."

"Stop. Don't deny you didn't feel it."

She turned her back to him to tidy the already neat contents of the changing table's shelves.

He stood close enough behind her to feel her heat.

Eyes closed, he imagined them in a different world—one where she finally told him the reason she'd torn them apart. He hadn't meant to confront her, but holding this baby brought it all rushing back—just how great they'd been together. How great they could be again, if only she'd let him in.

But did he really even want that?

Or had last night's buzz combined with the sweet smell of fresh-washed baby hair messed with his head?

"You know what?" Grady spun on his heel to aim for the door. "Forget I asked. It was stupid, and I didn't mean it. Clearly, I need to lay off the suds, and I apologize if I made you feel uncomfortable. So…" He forced a deep breath, and nodded toward the baby. "That said, you go on to work, and know I've got this."

He'd reached the door and had his hand on the knob before she said, "Grady, wait…"

Mouth dry, he couldn't wait.

He couldn't talk to her. He couldn't look at her.

He couldn't trust himself not to reveal any more of himself than he already had. It was embarrassing—the way he'd mooned over her when his guard had been down. And so he opened the door, sidestepping a curious Cotton on his way down the hall and away from the woman who'd proved to be his own personal kryptonite.

Shell-shocked. That was the only way Jessie could describe how she felt after what just happened with Grady. Who was she fooling? He knew she'd wanted to kiss him. Even all these years later, he didn't just hold the power to get in her head—he was still in her soul. How did she fix that? How did she once and for all exorcise him, since he sure couldn't stay?

Though she'd secretly wanted nothing more than to spend the day with Grady and their sweet little mystery baby, she was already late for work at a school that no longer existed, which was no doubt the reason she'd been hateful to him from the moment he'd opened his eyes— piercing blue eyes that made her think of an endless blue sky, and all the times she'd lost herself staring into them.

She didn't feel like facing another day of sifting through rubble any more than she felt like marching down the stairs to face Grady, but how could she call herself a teacher and not even be brave enough to give her old high school flame a solid answer as to why she hadn't wanted to kiss him? Maybe because any form of denial would be an absolute lie?

Disgusted with herself and this whole situation, she changed from sweats and a vintage Shania concert T-shirt into khaki shorts and last year's school field day T-shirt. She accessorized with thick socks and hiking boots— just what she wanted for dressing to impress her parents' houseguest.

Clomping down the stairs got Cotton all wound up, but thankfully didn't upset the baby.

She found Grady seated on the sofa with the infant lounging in the crook of his left arm, intently staring at him while he read aloud from some technical manual in a silly singsong voice.

"'Be cautioned not to set decompression limits outside your optimal—'" He caught sight of her and stopped. "Have a good day. Hope you find lots of good stuff."

Not caring if she was late, Jessie sat on the opposite end of the sofa and primly crossed her legs. "Since we're both adults, and too old for playing games, when we were sitting at the bar and you leaned in close, I thought you were going to kiss me and I was ready." *Dying for it.* "But then you backed away. Worse yet, you traipsed off to the dance floor with that chick who used to be in our fourth-hour Spanish class."

"That's where I knew her from." He smacked his forehead.

He was infuriating to the point that she wished the Think About Good Decisions time-out corner in her former classroom could be utilized by grown-ups who failed to follow her rules. Only that wouldn't be entirely fair. Considering she was the one who'd broken his heart.

Jessie cleared her throat. "As I was saying, your move at the bar confused me, so when you tried it again on the dance floor, I believed the beer was directing your actions and not you."

"What are you saying? If we'd both been stone sober, you would have green-lighted our kiss?"

"No." *Yes!* She covered her superflushed face with her hands. "Maybe. I don't know what I'm saying, other than I'm sorry I hurt you."

"And here we are, seven endless years later, right back at the heart of the matter. Tell me, Jess. Did my breath or feet stink? For all the years we were together, did you secretly think I was a bad kisser? Was my goal of becoming a rancher like my dad not good enough? Did you have your sights set on becoming a doctor's wife? Once and for all put me out of my misery and tell me *why.* All I need to move on is that one simple answer. You owe me that much."

She hung her head. Yes, she did owe him an answer. But was now the time or place?

"Jess, *please*…"

I want to tell you, Grady.

More than anything in the world, she wanted not only to tell him the truth, but to have him be okay with it, and to tell her he didn't mind never having the son or daughter that he'd talked about—*dreamed* about—for as long as she'd known him. But that wasn't likely to happen. Moreover, she would never allow him to give that dream up. Not after seeing what an amazing father he would make, judging by the ten minutes he'd spent caring for their mystery baby.

"Jess…" He set the baby on the cushion beside him, penning her safely in before standing, only to kneel in front of Jessie, bracing his strong, warm palms on her knees. When their stares locked, she looked away. "What's so awful that you can't tell me? What the hell are you trying to hide?"

A teary gasp escaped Jessie's aching throat as she wrenched free of Grady's hold to grab her purse and keys before dashing for her car.

"Jess!"

Grady stood at the front door, cradling the baby in his arms. He looked so strong and capable and handsome that it took every shred of willpower not to leave her car and run to him, begging him to give her a second chance despite the fact that she was damaged goods. But that would not only be wrong, but cruel.

He deserved to be a dad.

As for what she deserved?

Eyes welling, Jessie backed out of the drive. Of course, she deserved happiness all her own, and one day, she'd find it—just not with Grady Matthews.

Chapter Six

"Damn it," Grady mumbled under his breath while watching Jessie drive away. The government hadn't invested big bucks into training him for nothing. He saw through Jessie's lies—trouble was, knowing she lied was one thing. Figuring out what the lie entailed was a whole different ball game.

Odds were, she hadn't found another guy, or she'd have been with him. She hadn't dumped him for a big-city career, or she wouldn't have gone to college just up the road from their small town, then moved right back upon earning her diploma. What the hell was left?

"Baby," he said to the infant as she suckled her knuckles while napping on his chest, "that woman's gonna be the death of me."

The little lady predictably had no comment.

Lord, what he wouldn't give to spend the rest of the day out riding fences or checking cattle or, hell, even mucking stalls. He just wanted to feel normal again.

"You need a name," he said to the baby before heading back inside. "I know it'll just be temporary, but how about I call you Angel?" He tweaked her adorable button nose. "Because no one but an angel could've survived what you went through."

She eked open her big blue eyes, took a moment to take him in, then launched right back into one of her full-blown wails.

"All right, I get it." He aimed for kitchen, hoping Jessie or Billy Sue had at least left him ample feeding supplies. "Apparently, your momma taught you the meaning of stranger danger from a young age. I can respect that."

He found a bottle and cans of premade formula, and as frantic as the infant had already grown, he figured his best course was to hold her while making her bottle.

"Hope you're hungry," he said in his most ridiculous high-pitched baby tone, "'cause if all of this fuss is because you're scared, we might have a problem."

Lucky for him, when he presented her with the bottle, she sucked greedily. Whew. Crisis averted.

A good thing, but also bad, since it gave his mind ample time to wander—something he didn't want it to do. He could spend days—hell, he literally had spent years—trying to figure out Jessie's big secret, but now that he was in town not just for a day or two over a holiday, but for a good long while, baby or not, he owed it to himself to once and for all get to the bottom of this whole mess before heading back to his real world.

Rock Bluff and his family and friends and the ranch used to be his world, but now literally all of it was gone. Oh, sure, the people remained, but they were displaced in his mind. None fit where his memory had neatly compartmentalized them to be. And that scared him. No matter what, in the darkest of war-torn places, he'd always had this idyllic town and his reminisces to come home to.

Now? Everything was just gone.

Sure, nothing could flat-out take away all the good

times he recalled, but faced with this new reality of what the small town had become, remembering the old was damn near impossible.

Tired of being inactive, Grady unearthed an infant safety seat and stroller in the garage, then packed up a diaper bag he'd found in the nursery. After a shower and dressing in cargo shorts, a T-shirt, socks and his trusty boots, he loaded his rental car, tucked Angel into her rear-facing seat and was good to go.

If possible, the sight of the elementary school was even more depressing than it had been the day before.

He couldn't even choose which noise was more annoying—the roar of forward-moving dozers, or the *beep, beep, beep* safety alert when they were backing up.

One of the treasures he'd found in the garage was a chest-hugging baby-pack, so he slipped his arms through and buckled the straps, then tucked Angel inside, where she looked around for a few moments, then promptly fell asleep.

He covered her blond curls with a sun hat.

"Your nap's probably a good call," he mumbled. "Wish I could sleep through this. Hopefully I'd wake back on base with it all having been a nightmare."

At only ten in the morning, the spring sun's heat was intense. Good for drying salvageable items from the wreckage. Bad for the folks out working in the rising temperature. The smell was a dank, dusty blend of chalky concrete and all things kid—pink erasers and paste and crayons and magic markers. Only all of it had been twisted and mashed and crushed together to produce an overpowering stench that had it been bottled would have worn the label Sad.

He picked his way through the debris of former classrooms, smiling and waving along the way to the few men and women he'd met the day before.

At Jessie's room, he paused on the former threshold, chest tight at the sight of her kneeling to pull a book out from under an overturned terrarium. She'd always been a softy for animals. What had been inside?

She looked up, and for a split second, her expression brightened, but then she resumed her frown. "Why would you bring the baby down here?"

"Because we have unfinished business. Plus, I figured you'd need the help."

"Thanks, but no thanks."

"Jess, stop. It's me. If you don't want to talk about last night, or why we broke up, I'll honor that wish." *For now.* "But don't let stubbornness get in the way of practicality." He gestured toward her desk chair. "You hold the baby for a while and let me power through some of this stuff."

For an awkward few seconds, he thought she would deny him, but then her eyes welled with tears and she nodded. "I hoped today would be better, you know? Since I was used to this new reality. But how do you ever really get used to seeing everything you once loved gone?"

Her statement was true on so many levels. Applicable to not just the tornado damage, but to the two of them.

He went to her, holding out his arms for a hug he feared she wouldn't step into. But she did, and for the longest time, with the sun bearing down on them, and the baby sandwiched between them, Jessie allowed Grady to hold her, and he was honored and relieved, and when she stepped away, even though he hated himself for it, he was still hungry for more.

JESSIE COULD HAVE stood there in the sun with Grady holding her for hours. But having the baby between them seemed like an incredibly cruel joke. It was as if she were being taunted. Here was everything she ever wanted—the man, the baby—finally in her arms. Only that was a lie, because she could rightfully claim neither. And that hurt.

"Thank you for coming," she said softly.

"You're welcome." He pulled the baby from her pouch, then handed her over.

"I'm all dirty," Jessie protested even as he held the infant against her.

"That's okay. A little dirt is good for kids. Makes 'em strong."

Though her throat still ached with unshed tears, she laughed, and found that to be far better than more crying. Whether Grady and this miracle baby were in her life for a few extra hours or days, why not enjoy whatever time they did share?

"Might not have been my place, but while you were gone, I named her Angel. What do you think?"

"Perfect."

An hour later, Jessie couldn't decide which sight better fed her soul—Angel's big blue eyes, or Grady's great big muscular chest. Vastly different images that brought on equally happy thoughts.

"We won't tell Grady," she whispered to the baby, "because it would only inflate his already plenty big ego, but he's grown even more handsome, hasn't he?"

The pediatrician Jessie's mom had taken Angel to had thought the infant's age to be between two to three months. In light of this fact, when all Jessie received in answer was a blob of drool, she took that as agreement.

"Have you been looking for this guy?" Grady held up Toby, the classroom box turtle her father had fished from the pool the previous summer. He'd been half-dollar-size then, but had since doubled. Accustomed to being handled, he didn't bother hiding. Instead, he stuck out his head and wriggled his feet, probably hoping for dinner.

"Oh, my gosh!" she said in an excited rush. "I thought he was gone." She leaped from her chair, tucking the baby onto her left hip to grab Toby, then delivered a spur-of-the-moment kiss to Grady's cheek. "Thank you."

"He's cute." Grady held out the red plastic bin she'd once used for storing papers needing to be graded. "How about stashing him in here since his house seemed to have suffered storm damage."

"Great plan." She set the turtle inside, then used the hand sanitizer from her purse before touching the baby. "Poor guy's probably starving. Let's head to the play-ground for grass and grubs."

"Yum."

A few minutes later, she placed the turtle on the ground beneath one of the few standing trees—an oak that'd probably been around long enough to have witnessed the Oklahoma Land Rush.

"Hard to believe we went to this same school," Grady said. "What's your boss say about rebuilding?"

"I don't think anyone's thought beyond finishing the school year. First Street Church survived intact, and they've offered to let us set up there for the last weeks. Thank goodness state testing's out of the way, so at least we don't have that to worry about."

"And all of your kids came out of this okay?"

She nodded. "We were lucky the storm hit after school

had been let out for the day. But it was rush hour. Rock Bluff might be small, but so many people who live here commute into Norman or Oklahoma City. My students are thankfully okay physically, but they've got to be shaken up. More than half my class lost their homes."

"Lord…" He shook his head.

"I don't even know where to start rebuilding my own life." She sat on the metal bench she'd last used while on recess duty. "No apartment, no job…"

"Hey…" He sat beside her, rubbing her back. "Your job's fine—only displaced. As for your apartment, just like the town and school, it'll be rebuilt—better than ever. Just think, fresh paint, new carpet and appliances. That's all good, right?"

She managed a half laugh while adjusting the baby's hat. "Sounds great—except for the part where I'm stuck with Billy Sue and Roger for God only knows how long until my new place gets built."

"I'd offer to let you crash with me, but I share with two other guys and you might not like the always empty fridge or testosterone."

"Thanks. I could deal with that, but the whole being-located-in-Virginia thing might make for a bitch of a commute."

"True. On the plus side, at least your folks have an abundance of free food and a great pool."

"A definite plus." She took the baby's tiny hand, inspecting her fingers. "Wonder if any progress has been made toward finding her parents."

"I'm sure not, or one of us would have been called."

"You're probably right."

He took a deep breath and sighed. "What now?"

"Since we've found about all there is in my room, how about a trek into Norman for a new turtle house?"

"Aw, IS THIS terrarium for your baby's first pet?" The white-haired pet shop clerk made a silly face at Angel, but even if the baby had been old enough for a big smile, the only look she seemed capable of was a vacant stare.

Grady said, "In a roundabout way."

"The baby's not ours," Jessie said. "We're watching her for friends."

"Oh." The woman nodded. "She's awfully cute. Your friends are blessed. Nothing brings a couple closer than a sweet new baby."

After clearing his throat, Grady asked, "Do you have any of those water bowls turtles can crawl in and out of?"

"Sure, in the next aisle over. I'll show you."

They found everything else they needed, then fought at the register over who would pay. Grady won.

They were in the car, halfway back to her parents' house when he said, "That was awkward."

"The thing about us being Angel's parents?"

"Yeah. Thanks for coming to my rescue. I wasn't sure what to say. I've only been with her a day, but I'm going to miss her, you know?"

"I sure do." She bowed her head. "I've thought about how hard it's going to be to say goodbye since we picked her up last night."

"We're a couple of screwups, huh? Both of us ready and willing to settle down, but no one can put up with either of us long enough to tie the knot."

"That's about the size of it."

He switched lanes to pass an RV. "Know what we should do?"

"Can't imagine."

"Have one of those marriage pacts. Say if in ten years, neither of us is involved, we'd still have each other. Voilà—problem solved."

"I can't believe you just said that."

"Don't get your panties in a wad. You know I'm messing with you—at least about the marriage pact."

"Still…" She folded her arms. "That's nothing to joke about."

"All kidding aside, more than anything, I want my own wife—family." *I want you, Jess.* He was tired of being alone. He'd stopped short of admitting that last fact because it was embarrassing. He was a grown-ass man who, back in Virginia, had women parading in and out of his place damn near every night, yet none of them made his pulse race the way Jess did.

"Me, too. I mean, well, someday I'd like to have a husband." She'd worried the cuticle on her right thumb until drawing a spot of blood. She took a tissue from her purse to press against it.

"Great. Then, we're in business." He tried making light of their impossible situation. "I'll have my lawyer draw up our marriage-pact papers."

"Please, stop." She pressed her fingertips to her forehead.

"Headache?"

"Yeah—you."

Chapter Seven

I could throttle him!

Late that night, after the rest of their exhausting ride home and endless pre- and post-dinner small talk with their families, Jessie had finally stolen a moment for herself on the covered swing by the dark pool.

Of course, Grady had no idea how his glib marriage talk had hurt. How could he?

But that didn't change the fact that while he'd joked about marriage, odds were, she'd never have that option. And that had never hurt more. With Grady back in her life—even temporarily—she could no longer hide from the possibilities of how wonderful a life with him would have been.

That afternoon, with Angel on her lap and Toby the turtle crawling on lush spring grass, Grady had said something—she couldn't even remember what—and time had stopped while she'd just stared at him, drinking him in. The strong set of his whisker-stubbled jaw. The way dappled sunlight glinted off the hint of red in his dark hair. The warm tingles from which she'd had to hide a shiver when he'd run his hand along her back. Oh, she knew his gesture had been friendly, but her body had misconstrued his intentions by craving more.

"Hiding?"

Jessie groaned inwardly.

"Grady, if you don't mind, I'd rather be alone."

"Why? Because I was a jackass this afternoon in the car? You don't think I noticed the cold chill you've given me ever since?"

"I haven't—"

"Sorry, okay? Please stop being a Sensitive Suzy."

"There you go again." How could he have been her dream man on the playground only to turn insensitive jerk by night? "Making light of an issue that's very painful to many women."

"You personally?" By pale moonlight, she witnessed his gaze narrow.

"No." She swallowed hard. "But lots of other women— and I'm not just talking about getting married, but having a family. My friend Gloria, who teaches third grade in the room next to mine—or at least used to—suffered horribly from infertility issues."

"Did she ever have a kid?"

"Well, yes. But it took her and her husband two years of trying. A few of the women in her support group still haven't conceived."

"I'm sorry to hear that." He took her hands. *Took her hands.* The gravity of this moment took time to fully sink in. After seven endless years of wondering what might have been, she and Grady sat alone in the moonlight with him touching her as sweetly as he ever had. But why? What was the point? Before her heart went and did something stupid like falling for him all over again, she jerked her hands free.

"What did I do now?"

"Nothing." She stood. "Just please stop touching me. We're not together anymore, and—"

Like that night at the bar, he leaned closer, and she leaned closer, desperately craving the kind of kiss that she sometimes, in the quiet of night, felt as if she'd waited a lifetime to experience again. Then suddenly, with his mouth mere inches from hers, Jessie was trapped between heaven and hell, knowing exactly what she wanted but could never have.

Never.

This was for his own good. Why couldn't he accept that fact?

She pushed him away, and when she ran, he let her— which hurt even worse, but for entirely different reasons. It hurt because that meant her message to him had finally sunk in, and he was following her advice to leave her alone.

Out of breath, she leaned against the still sun-warm bricks at the back of the house and held her hands over her aching heart. She forced deep breaths, reminding herself that all she had to do was ride this out and in a little over a week he'd be gone. She'd resume teaching, and aside from her apartment, life would be back to normal.

All of that sounded so good on the surface, but what she feared as she inched her hands up to cover her stupid needy lips was that the emotional damage Grady had just unwittingly inflicted with all that talk about marriage hurt far worse than what had been done by the actual storm.

MIDMORNING THE NEXT DAY, the sun blazed down on Grady's long-sleeved denim shirt. If there hadn't been so much fiberglass insulation tossed like cotton candy around his parents' ranch, he'd have just taken it off.

The heat worsened his already sour mood.

He adjusted his battered straw cowboy hat to shade his eyes from the worst of the glare.

As hard as the work was, at least it got his mind off Jessie and that damned kiss he'd wanted but hadn't gotten. But there she was, popping right back into his head. The woman was a bigger mystery than Bigfoot, crop circles and UFOs all combined into one.

Once the insurance money came through, his folks would hire a crew to rebuild the house and barn, but in the meantime, Grady's father had enlisted his help in cleaning debris from the pasture closest to the house, then sprucing up one of the older outbuildings that had survived relatively unscathed to use as a temporary shelter for the chickens and horses.

With so many fences down, the cattle had scattered. All three horses were accounted for, but not happy. They were a spoiled lot, and accustomed to sleeping in their cozy barn.

Most of the chickens were penned, but stubborn holdouts still roosted in the yard's few remaining trees.

"Dad?" Grady tossed a wayward piece of corrugated metal onto the trash pile.

"Yeah?" He spit juice from his chewing tobacco.

"Have you ever done something you're not real proud of, but at the same time wouldn't take back?"

"Depends. We talking about ranching?"

"Women."

His dad chuckled. "Considering how long me and your momma have been hitched, I'd have to go a long ways back to recall anything like that."

"Can you try?" He pitched a toilet seat and what he thought was the bottom half of his mom's hot curler hair thingies.

"Well, I guess there was this one time when your momma got a bee in her bonnet about wanting to take a break. I wasn't even sure what that meant, but my friends all said that was girl code for saying she technically wanted to break things off, but keep me off-limits to any other gals. That didn't set right with me, so that weekend, me and my boys went to a rodeo down in Duncan. You know how rodeos are—dang near as many pretty girls as horses. We got settled in the stands alongside a giggly bunch from Chickasha, one thing led to another and next thing I knew, the rodeo was over and we were all out in one of the girl's daddy's pasture, drinking beer and lookin' up at the stars. The gal I was with—Becky, I think was her name—snuggled real close, and I was so sore at your momma that I kissed the fool out of that little gal, and liked it. Come Monday, your momma tucked a note in my school locker, telling me how sorry she was and that she wanted to get back together. I agreed and we've been paired up ever since." He tipped his hat back and spit. "Never told your momma about that gal, and I'd hope you wouldn't, either."

"No, sir. I won't."

"So what's my ancient history got to do with you and Jessie Long?"

"I tried kissing her—twice."

"And…?"

"Both times, I got the distinct impression she wanted to be kissed, but then she went and acted all huffy, as if she didn't."

"Hmm…" He pitched a branch and a sofa cushion. "Whatever happened between you two?"

"Good question. One day, I thought we were gonna talk wedding dates. The next, she tells me it's over. I thought I was done even thinking about her, but being back here, watching her with that baby in her arms… It's dredged up a whole bunch of muck from the bottom of my pond."

"What're you gonna do about it?"

"Beats me." Grady found a framed family photo taken during a Christmas back when both sets of his grandparents had been alive. It needed a good scrubbing, but was otherwise in good shape. He set it on what they'd established as the "keeper" shelf. "I've tried finding someone else, but I only want her. She's like a long-lasting poison ivy or mess of chigger bites—annoying as hell and refusing to go away. At least, in my head. In real life, just like back in high school, she wants nothing to do with me. Hell, in Virginia, I'm turning gals away. But here, Jessie acts like I'm hunchbacked and covered in warts."

His dad busted out laughing.

"It's not funny."

"Sorry. I just can't help but wonder if she's pulling the same kind of stunt your momma did. You know, taking a *break*?" He spit.

"It's been seven freaking years. That's one helluva break."

"Tell you what…" He took a long drink from the ice-water jug Grady's mother had sent with them. "I was going to ask if you wanted to help me round up the cattle this weekend. Take a tent and have a cookout and make a nice time out of it. But what if you and Jess went instead?" He winked and grinned. "I'll be the first one to tell you that all manner of good things happen under the stars—just don't tell your momma."

"No," JESSIE SAID that night during dinner when Grady asked her on an overnight campout to round up cattle—right in front of her mom and dad and his parents and even baby Angel, whom she held in the crook of her left arm. "I've got way too much to do around here."

"Like what?" her meddlesome mother asked. "Rose and I are plenty capable of caring for the baby and your turtle, and anyway, I'm sure Angel's parents will be found just any time. Go on, get out of here. The fresh air will do you good."

"If you don't want to take horses," Grady said, "Allen offered to let us use their four-wheelers."

"You love four-wheeling," her father said. "Remember when we rented them down in Mexico and you had so much fun we rode two days in a row?"

"I said no, and I mean it." Jessie tossed her napkin to the dining room table and charged to her room with Angel staring at her, wide-eyed. She'd have preferred going outside, but it was raining.

In her room, with the door closed behind her, Jessie laid Angel on the bed, then opened the hatch door in Toby's new terrarium to feed him a cricket.

Then she did something she should have done years earlier—removed the delicate silver chain she wore with Grady's engagement ring.

After tucking it into her jewelry box for safekeeping, she climbed onto her childhood bed, resting Angel on the pillow alongside her. "Do they all think I'm stupid? That I can't see what they're trying to do?"

Angel gurgled.

"Stop being so cute," Jessie said with a sad smile. "You're not helping."

A knock sounded on the door.

She tensed in anticipation of it being her mother in scolding mode for being rude. Worse yet would be Grady. But then, when had he ever knocked?

"Come in," Jessie said begrudgingly.

The door opened, and she was shocked to see Grady's sweet-tempered mother. "It's just me. Mind if I come in?"

"Rose. Hi." Jessie sat up in the bed, suddenly self-conscious. As a teen, she'd spent hours in the woman's kitchen, baking, swapping stories, sharing family meals. After the breakup, she'd mourned the loss of Grady's warmhearted family nearly as much as him. He was their only son, and according to Billy Sue, Rose had struggled when he'd left for the Navy. "Please come in."

"I don't mean to intrude. I could just tell you were upset, and I know we haven't *really* visited in a while, but I hope you won't mind letting an old woman have her say?"

"You're hardly old, Rose. You and Mom both beat Corny and me in that Glow Run 5k."

"True, but I ached all over for a week after." Rose tentatively sat in the armchair tucked alongside the dresser. Perched on just the edge, she looked poised to bolt. "Downstairs, after you left the table, so did my Grady." She forced a deep breath. "No one much talks about boys having broken hearts—oh, not that Grady's a boy anymore, but you know what I mean. Guess he'll always be a boy to me. When you broke things off with him, I was genuinely scared for him. Neither Ben nor I had ever seen him so...*dark*. When he joined the Navy, made that fancy SEAL team, we were so proud. Beyond that, we were excited for him to finally get a fresh start. Please don't think I'm mentioning all of this to make you feel bad—believe it or not, I used to be your age, and remember how crazy those first heady stages of love can make you feel. But now that I've been married a while, that love has changed. It's transformed from rushing rapids to a lazy flow, but it's still there, deep and rich and full of life." She paused as if carefully searching for her next words. "When you think no one's looking, I've seen the way you moon over Grady. Goes without saying, he does the same with you."

Jessie closed her eyes and wished the woman would go away.

"In just over a week, my boy's leaving again, and I don't know when he'll be back…i-if *ever*." Her words caught in her throat. "I have to be a realist, and the reality is that he's a soldier. Good men die in bad places all the time. You don't have to decide right now, but promise me you'll at least sleep on the notion of going on that campout with my son. With every bone in my body, I know you two are perfect for each other. There has to be a reason you're not together. Please, for Grady—for *yourself*—take these two days and once and for all get to the heart of what's kept you apart."

Rose left as quietly as she'd entered, but her words resonated in Jessie's heart. As much as she loved the woman, she tried her best to shut out Rose's message. But when Grady's mom reminded her of the fact that in his capacity as a soldier, every time Grady left on one of his missions, he stood the very real risk of not coming back, terror lodged in her throat.

Just thinking about last night—how they'd almost

kissed—returned an excited rush that carried with it secret shame. Of course she wanted to be with Grady. All these years later, that desire had never stopped. But that didn't change her infertility, or the fact that he wanted a family. Still, if he was willing to joke about getting his wife from something as unconventional as a marriage pact, who was to say he might not be opposed to alternative means of having kids? If so, why couldn't they pursue that avenue together?

For the first time in forever, hope welled deep, blossoming just like the world around her. So many storms had brought her down, but what if the tragedy that had returned Grady to Rock Bluff—to her—turned out to have a silver lining?

GRADY DIDN'T MAKE it back to the house until after midnight.

His initial inclination had been to head straight for the Dew Drop and drink himself into a better mood, but he still had a job to do in the morning rounding up his dad's cattle whether Jessie accompanied him or not.

As such, he'd driven to the ranch.

Spending his evening with the horses was preferable to being around Jessie. The gal reminded him of a cactus—all prickly on the outside, but soft and tender just beyond the thorns. He never should have tried kissing her, but how was he ever supposed to get past her sharp exterior without a little reminding of how good they used to be?

Given his choice, he'd have slept on a horse blanket beneath the stars, but come morning, he was borrowing Roger's camping equipment and still had to run to a store for provisions. So when his eyelids felt heavier than air, he climbed back in his rental to drive to the Longs'.

He'd just crept through the dark house, thankful that yappy Cotton slept with Billy Sue behind her closed door, when Jessie scared the bejeezus out of him by stepping out from the nursery to block his bedroom door.

She held Angel in her arms.

The rain had passed.

Moonlight spilled through the window at the end of the hall, casting both girls in a fanciful net. They didn't even look real. Jessie wore her hair down—long and wavy—just the way he favored. Her short white PJ set didn't leave much to the imagination and as he stood there staring, her nipples hardened. She could deny her attraction to him all she wanted, but her body apparently couldn't lie.

The fact that she held a sleeping infant on her hip only made her that much more attractive, that much easier to envision as his wife. Lord, they'd have an amazing life together—building the house they'd always wanted, working the land and cattle all week, then holding hands and sharing Indian tacos at rodeos on Friday and Saturday nights.

But for this fantasy to come true, was he willing to give up all he'd worked for in becoming a SEAL?

Maybe...

The rest of his life depended on her.

"We need to talk," she said, effectively breaking the spell.

Chapter Eight

Now that Jessie had Grady in front of her, she wasn't sure what to say. Her mouth had grown dry and her tongue felt thick. He represented everything in her life she'd been missing. Companionship and security and fun. But for her to find all of that meant he had to give something up.

"Well?" he said. "You wanted to talk?"

Her plan to throw caution to the wind and tell him everything now seemed silly—moreover, selfish.

"Look, I've apologized for trying to kiss you. I was wrong, and shouldn't have—"

On her tiptoes, Jessie kissed him quiet. "I'm not mad at you for *trying* to kiss me, but because you *didn't* kiss me. Oh—and I'll go with you tomorrow."

"Just like that?" His gaze narrowed. "What changed?"

Nothing. Everything. Even their brief kiss still tingled on her lips. "I'm not sure. I just think getting out of here for a little while will do me good. If, in the process, I can help your parents get back on their feet, all the better."

"I'm getting an early start."

"You know I'm a morning person."

The set of his mouth unexpectedly grim, he nodded. "Okay, well, did you want to use horses or four-wheelers?"

"Horses. Still have Misty, Fred and Freckles?"

"Yep. Let me guess—you want Misty?"

Though he still frowned, Jessie smiled. "Us girls need to stick together."

JESSIE HAD SET HER alarm for five. She made blueberry muffins for breakfast and snacks, hearty ham sandwiches for lunch and frozen beef stew fixings for her mom's Dutch oven for dinner.

By the time Grady rolled out of bed at six, as far as the food portion of their trek was concerned, she had all the bases covered.

"You weren't kidding about still being a morning person. Thanks. I was just planning on grabbing a few cans of pork and beans."

She rolled her eyes. "Where's the fun in that?"

"Okay…" He bowed his head and half laughed while running his hands through his hair. "Before I take you anywhere, what gives? What's with this one-eighty in your attitude?"

"Let's just say you owe your mom a hug."

He groaned. "What the hell does my mom have to do with this? Did she go to you and, like, promise a plate of cookies if you'd give her pathetic son a mercy date? Lord…"

"Stop. It wasn't like that at all."

"Then, what was it like, Jess? Because right about now, I'm feeling—"

"Good morning," Billy Sue sang out. She held Angel in her arms. "I went to check on this little darling, and she was already awake, just staring up at her mobile. She's got a big day today."

"How so?" Jessie sidestepped glowering Grady to pack utensils and salt and pepper.

"She's having a new set of photos taken that will go out to police stations nationwide—on the off chance that her parents were just passing through, and there's family somewhere out there who might recognize her. Then, this afternoon, we're going on *Oklahoma Today* to help spread the word."

"Good." Jessie added napkins to her already bulging canvas knapsack. "It's crazy to me that her parents still haven't stepped forward." She smoothed the baby's downy curls. "If she were mine, I'd move heaven and earth to find her."

Grady cleared his throat. "Anyone considered that Angel's parents might be dead?"

"No," both women said at once.

Billy Sue took a formula can from the cabinet next to the fridge. "Grady, while I accept your question as a possibility, let's not go down that road just yet."

"Whatever you say." He nodded toward the bag Jessie had packed. "This ready to go?"

"Yes, please. Let me grab my backpack, and I'll help load the rest of the gear."

"Thanks." Without even a backward glance, he left for the garage.

Billy Sue asked, "Who peed in his Wheaties?"

"Mom!" Jessie couldn't help but laugh. "Do you talk to your constituents with that mouth?"

"Yes, ma'am. The good ol' boys down at the Waffle Hut love it when I get sassy." She winked. "Now, what's with Grady's mood? And when you're done explaining that, last I heard you weren't camping. Not that I'm complaining, but what's with the sudden change of heart?"

"We'll talk later. I don't have time now." She kissed Angel's chubby pink cheek. "Bye, sweetheart. Enjoy your TV debut." To her mom, she said, "Be sure you record the show. I want to see her in all her TV-star glory."

"What about me?"

Jessie kissed her, too. "Goes without saying that you'll steal the show."

After a jog upstairs for her backpack and to feed Toby—Cotton barking and nipping at her heels the whole way—Jessie escaped outside and went to look for Grady in the garage. Didn't matter whether he was ready to go or not. She was ready to escape her mother's nosy questions. How could she explain any of this to her mom when she didn't even fully understand why she was accompanying Grady?

"I've still got a few minutes to go." He unearthed a sleeping bag from beneath a pile of Christmas decorations.

"That's okay. What can I do to help?" The straw cowboy hat he'd bought for her fifteenth birthday hung from a peg on the far wall, alongside her dad's six golf hats and snow-skiing goggles.

She took her hat and slapped it on her head.

Two seconds later, it felt as if an eight-legged creature moseyed along her scalp.

She shrieked, then flung the hat off, wildly waving at her hair. "Get it off! Get it off!"

Grady flew to her side, only to shake his head. "Is that what caused all the fuss?" Grinning, he pointed at a daddy longlegs spider as it crawled under the lawn mower.

"It's not funny." She inspected inside the hat's crown to make sure nothing else had set up residence.

"Everything okay?" Billy Sue stood in the doorway with Angel.

"Fine," Grady said. "The way Jessie was hollering, I thought a rattler was in her hat, but it was only a spider."

"Ew!" She shivered. "Spiders are just as bad."

"Agreed." Jessie checked her arms and legs—just in case.

"Grady," Billy Sue asked, "how many head of cattle does your father have roaming around?"

"A hundred and seventy-three accounted for in the north and east pastures, but another seventy-two missing in the west. There's a lot of forested places to hide in there, and he's guessing the calves and mommas went in there to find shelter from the storm."

"Gracious…" Billy Sue shook her head. "Is there no end to the damage this tornado has done? We're still missing twenty-three souls within city limits—another twelve in the outlying areas." She hugged Angel extra-close. "I don't even want to think about what may have happened to this little lady's folks."

Grady carried a Coleman lantern to his rental's open trunk.

"Why aren't you taking your dad's truck?" Billy Sue asked.

Jessie elbowed her in an attempt to get her to march her nosy behind back inside.

"Ouch," her loudmouthed mom complained. "What'd you do that for?"

Jessie rolled her eyes before hiding her superheated cheeks behind the ruse of further inspecting her hat.

"Ma'am," Grady said to Billy Sue, "while Jess and

I are out riding, Mom and Dad will be at what's left of the house, seeing what all's salvageable. They rented a storage unit in Norman, so I figure they may need the truck to make a few trips."

"Oh, sure," Billy Sue nodded. "Roger and I rode along the day you two found Toby."

"Don't forget to feed him," Jessie reminded.

Grady added her backpack and one she presumed to be his own to his car "We're good to go."

"So soon?" Billy Sue used her free hand to fan herself. "Grady, you are a wonder. Strong, fast, brave *and* handsome—the total package."

"Mom!" Jessie whispered under her breath. Her cheeks burned hot enough to have been Crayola red. She gave her mother a goodbye hug, then whispered into her ear, "What're you trying to do?"

Her mom laughed. "Duh—find you a big, strapping husband."

After saying their goodbyes to not only her mom, but Roger, Ben, Rose and Angel, then getting settled in the car, Jessie couldn't tell if Grady genuinely hadn't heard her mother's ridiculous comment or was just being polite. In case it was the latter, she said, "Sorry about that. Sometimes Mom gets carried away."

"Don't sweat it. I'm still pissed at my mother for whatever she said to get you on this trip."

"Promise, as usual, she was supersweet. It's crazy how different our two moms are. Half the time mine acts as if she's starring in her own reality show, while yours is unassuming and kind."

He laughed as he pulled onto the main road. "She didn't used to be so kind when giving me hell about finishing my homework and chores."

"You know what I mean." She caught her breath when she looked his way in time to catch his nodding smile. The sun hadn't risen anywhere near full strength and the lazy rays backlit him in gold.

"Yeah, I do. I love my job, but really miss my folks."

"Ever think about retiring from the Navy?"

"Sometimes—after an especially tough mission. But then ranch life isn't all that easy. Seemed as though with every ice storm we were out traipsing through pastures for mommas calving. Hay baling is always a joy. Then there's inoculation and castrations, when it's a damn near certainty someone's getting a hoof shiner."

Jessie nodded. "Remember that year my dad helped, so he'd be first in line for your mom's famous mountain oysters? He had a black eye for nearly two weeks."

Their shared laughter felt good. Comfortable and familiar and right.

He was quiet for a few moments as he turned onto the dirt road leading to the ranch and then he said, "I don't know about you, but how tough was it saying goodbye to Angel when there's a good chance she'll be gone when we get back?"

"I know, right?" Eyes instantly stinging, Jessie nodded. "I was trying not to think about it, but the whole time wondering the same. I mean, I hope all these new efforts do find her parents—she deserves a happy reunion. But it's crazy how attached I've become in such a short time."

"No kidding."

This time when her eyes stung, her throat knotted, too.

She faced the window to wipe silent tears with the long sleeves of her pink calico shirt. Even knowing motherhood would never happen for her, she'd imagined the wonder of that scene too many times to count. Each daydream devastated her a little more.

Thankfully, they shared a companionable silence for the remainder of the fifteen-minute ride.

At the ranch, ground-hugging fog swirled over the gently rolling hills, glowing in the morning sun. The spring air smelled clean and rich with loamy earth, wildflowers and tender grasses.

Approaching the horses, she'd forgotten how peaceful it was out here. The stillness accentuated every sound—the crunch of their boots on the dirt drive. A horse's neigh. Chickens' throaty gurgles and a woodpecker's knock. Despite the house and barn's devastation, the core beauty of the place hadn't changed.

"This is…" Hands on her hips, she stared out at the land that, for as far as the eye could see and farther, Grady's family owned, and she smiled. "Well, words don't seem adequate, but it's spellbinding. Crazy beautiful."

"Yeah…" He stood behind her, close enough that his radiant heat warmed her back the way the rising sun warmed her face. She longed for him to wrap his arms around her, drawing her into an embrace, nuzzling her neck, maybe then giving her a slow spin to face him so they might share a proper kiss. "The only good thing about leaving for months is that it seems more gorgeous every time I come back."

They stood there for a long moment—not touching, but close enough for her to yearn for him to pull her into his arms. Too bad she'd long ago turned him away. Since talking with Rose, she'd done a lot of soul-searching, and the only conclusion she'd reached was that she should have told him everything. Then let him decide if he still wanted to be with her. The fact that after all this time neither had moved on had to mean something.

"We should probably get going."

"O-okay." They'd stood there for so long, staring out at the rolling hills and fog-shrouded grazing cattle, that she'd forgotten their purpose—not to reconnect, but to do a job.

It had been a while since she'd saddled a horse, so Grady jumped in to help, ensuring she'd tightened the cinch so that it was snug around the horse's belly. In the process, all of his accidental brushes against her culminated in an achy longing to touch him deliberately, to smooth her fingers along those rippled abs her forearm had skimmed, or the hard chest she'd backed into. The whole scene played games with her mind. The rich scents of leather and horseflesh and faintly sweet manure all combined, evoking memories of the last time they'd ridden together. It had been nearly a decade, but those smells served as a time machine, transporting her back to when they'd have completed this preride ritual with kissing and laughing and copped feels that led to naughty strokes.

Now Grady was all business.

Only in her mind was everything all mixed up.

When it came time to mount Misty, Grady settled his hands low on Jessie's hips to help. Was she imagining the fact that she felt each individual fingertip blazing her skin through her jeans?

Grady mounted his horse, then took a crudely drawn map from the chest pocket of his faded denim shirt. "The west pasture is unfortunately the biggest—not really one pasture per se, but at least a dozen smaller ones that are surrounded by forest. Dad and I have cut trails through, but they're probably overgrown. We've got so much ground to cover that I made a search grid for us to follow. We'll shoot for a little over half today, stay the night at the old campsite in the middle sector at say 1800 hours, get some shut-eye, then finish off tomorrow. Sound doable?"

"Um, sure." Disappointment at his all-business demeanor clenched her stomach. What had she expected? For them to hold hands while riding off into the sunset when it was barely past seven in the morning?

Though she nudged Misty forward, Jessie couldn't help but feel as though she and Grady had taken a giant leap backward.

RIDING TO THE first forested area he planned to search, Grady couldn't shake the feeling that he'd been manipulated. The notion that the only reason Jessie had accompanied him was because of his mother's pity nursed what had been irritation into a full-on rage. What the hell? He was a freaking Navy SEAL—at the top of his game mentally and physically. The last thing he needed was his momma's help in finding a date.

He stewed while he rode, hoping Fred's rhythmic walk combined with plenty of fresh air and wide-open views would calm him, but no such luck.

Even after rescuing a calf from a mud hole and driving six heifers from a deep-forest glade back into one of the main western pastures, he couldn't shake his gnawing sense of unease.

"You're awfully quiet," Jessie said when they'd stopped for lunch at the property's highest point. Out of all the places he'd been in the world, this Oklahoma prairie view moved him most. Rolling pastures dotted with forest and crowned by limitless sky. Growing up on this ranch, he'd felt as if anything were possible—anything, it turned out, but getting hitched and sharing this amazing land with a family all his own.

"You didn't have to come, you know." Grady took the sandwich she'd offered and sat on the same flat rock he'd enjoyed since the first time he could remember his dad bringing him up here as a little boy.

"I wanted to." She bit into her sandwich and chewed. "Remember when we came up here to fly a kite, but the wind was blowing so hard it yanked it out of our hands?"

He couldn't help but chuckle. "It's probably still circling the globe. Lord, I was pissed. I paid two months' allowance for that thing."

"I'm sorry. You scowled almost as much back then as you have today. What's wrong?"

Where did he begin?

"You're not still mopey about that talk I had with your mother, are you? Because that would just be silly."

"Silly?" He lost a few notches on his man card even saying the word. "The fact that it took my mom to get you out here speaks volumes about where the two of us stand."

She set down her sandwich, sidling alongside him on his flat, sun-warmed rock. "I wouldn't be here if I didn't want to be."

"But that's just it. Why do you all of a sudden want to be? At the table last night, you were pretty adamant about staying as far from me as possible."

"Okay…" She forced a deep breath. "You really want to know why I'm here? Your mom said something unsettling."

Grady set his sandwich on his lap, covering his face with his hands. "This keeps getting worse. In fact—" he fished his keys from his pocket and handed them to her "—how about you just head back to the car, and pick me up in a few days."

"Stop. You sound like a big old grumpy bear with a thorn in his paw."

"Right. 'Cause we have so many grizzlies around here."

"You know what I mean. Your mom told me that every time you leave on one of your missions, she's scared to death you won't come back. When that sank in, it occurred to me that no matter how far away you are…" Brown eyes welling, she pressed her palm to her chest. "I always carry you in my heart. If something happened to you…" She bowed her head. "I'm not sure I could handle it."

"Cut the crap." He sighed, then stood, losing himself in the view, and his sandwich to the tall grass. "If the only reason you tagged along is because I might die, I'd rather you not be here at all. I could die falling off my horse, or hell, you could've died in that twister. What does our inevitable mortality have to do with anything?"

"You know what I meant. I wanted to be with you."

"Just in case? Would that ease your conscience if I take a bullet, Jess? Knowing that at least you spent quality time with me before my untimely demise?"

"Stop twisting my words. You're making me out to be some horrible person when all I wanted was to…"

"*What*, Jess?" When her words trailed off, he spun to face her, giving her shoulders a light shake. "What the hell do you want? You clearly don't want a relationship. Best as I can tell, most days, you don't even want to be my friend. You also don't want me to kiss you. I used to be pretty good at baseball, and best as I can recall, three *don'ts* makes me out."

Hoping to blow off steam, he released her to pace.

Her silence made him feel about two feet tall, and he was done. If she didn't want to be with him—fine. He'd finally gotten her message loud and clear.

"Come on, Fred. We've got work to do." He stroked the chestnut's mane.

"Grady, wait…" She tossed her sandwich after his.

"Why, Jess? Why should I spend one more second of my life waiting when it's clear all we used to share that was special is gone?"

Chapter Nine

Tell him! Jessie's conscience pleaded. *Tell him about your endometriosis, and how you'd give* anything *to be with him, but can't—for his own good.* How ever since she'd broken things off with him, a part of her had been not just broken, but missing.

Maybe if he knew, this wall between you would crumble, and you'd have a shot at once again being together.

The notion sounded great in theory, but the reality of sharing her darkest secret with him was even more terrifying than that tornado's roar. The true fear wasn't so much in the telling, but waiting for his reaction. Those few seconds between learning if he'd be supportive or turn her away would be the longest of her life. Just thinking about it made her pulse quicken uncomfortably and her palms sweat.

Tell him!

"Swell." Grady nudged his horse forward. "A few more minutes of my life wasted. Follow or don't, Jess. Either way, I've got work to do."

She should have called out to him again, but what was the point? Fear had stolen her ability to speak or think or do anything other than dwell on what might have been.

On what could be.

That morning, while baking blueberry muffins and packing their meals, hope had blossomed in her, as tender and fleeting as a spring flower. She'd put the cruel reality of her situation from her mind, to pretend her diagnosis didn't matter. Nothing had mattered other than making things right with Grady.

So why had everything between them never felt more wrong than it did now?

It had been eons since she'd ridden, and she embarrassingly couldn't climb into her saddle without help, so she led Misty to the rock where she and Grady had shared at least part of their lunch, then used it as a step stool to hoist herself onto the horse.

After a five-minute gallop, she caught up with Grady, and the two of them spent the rest of the day working side by side in silence. It didn't matter that he wasn't speaking to her. His quiet only strengthened her resolve to tell him everything tonight.

She'd wait until they'd settled around a cozy campfire and darkness had fallen, so that if his expression registered disappointment she wouldn't be able to see it.

By the time they'd located forty-three of the seventy-two missing cows and calves, the sun hung low and streaked the sky with orange and violet.

"Beautiful sunset, huh?"

Grady just grunted while removing Fred's saddle and then blanket.

Muscles aching, she followed suit with Misty.

With both horses brushed and contentedly grazing, she nodded toward the pile of camping gear. "What can I do to help?"

"Nothing." Grady and his dad had used the camping spot for years. Sheltered by six sturdy oaks, it was within earshot of a bubbling, spring-fed brook and featured a fire pit and benches carved from giant, six-foot logs.

"Grady…shouldn't I at least get firewood? I've got Mom's Dutch oven in my knapsack and all the fixings for beef stew."

"Not hungry."

"Would you stop being a stubborn old mule and talk to me?" She'd raised her voice enough that Fred bobbed his head and neighed.

"Got nothing to say." He shook the small, unassembled tent from its canvas bag.

"Great." She forced a deep breath. "Then, I guess it's lucky I have enough to say for both of us. I wanted to tell you this under more congenial circumstances, but…" The fact that her runaway pulse was on the verge of making her black out and he couldn't have cared less incensed her. "Can you please at least give me the courtesy of putting that down and looking my way?"

He dropped the metal stake he'd been holding, then sat back on his haunches. "What?"

She licked suddenly dry lips with an even drier tongue. "About our breakup— The reason…" Head bowed, Jessie wasn't sure this was such a good idea given Grady's dour mood.

"Whoa—*our* breakup? No. Let's not get this twisted. You ruined us, Jess. It was all you."

"Okay, fine. But I had a reason."

"So you say, but I have yet to hear it."

"God, for two seconds could you please be nice to me? I have endometriosis, okay?"

He narrowed his eyes. "What's that? Some kind of cancer?"

"No. It's not cancer. Long story short, it makes it so

I can't have kids. That's why I broke our engagement, Grady. Because that big family you've always wanted? Well, with me, you'll never have it."

Hands to his forehead, in the day's waning light, he looked dazed. When he hadn't moved for an endless few minutes, her stomach knifed in pain. This was it. Her worst fears coming true. He was so crushed by her diagnosis that he couldn't even look at her.

The knot at the back of her throat grew unbearable and she gasped from the effort of holding back tears.

Say something! she longed to scream.

He rose, then slipped his hands from his forehead to his mouth, then to his forehead again. "You're kidding," he finally said.

Seriously? That was the best he could do? "Why in the world would I *kid* about something that has defined my entire adult life? Any relationship I even try to forge is ruined before it begins. What guy in his right mind doesn't want to one day have his own son or daughter? Especially you. Lord knows, you talk about it enough."

"Jess..." He finally lowered his hands, only to raise them, clamping them on top of his head. "I'm sad for you—that's awful, but I'm also pissed. Like, what the hell? I *loved* you. I would have walked to hell and back for you. So why in the world would you not only face something like that alone, but also shut me out—the guy who put you first, before *anything* else? Why didn't you give me enough credit to do the right thing in staying by you—no matter what?"

The tears she'd held since the day he'd left for basic finally spilled—hot and silent in messy streams.

"Hell, Jess, did it ever once occur to you that we

could've adopted or gone the surrogacy route or bought a damned dog?"

"Y-you'd *never* be okay with just a d-dog, Grady! For as long as I've known you, all you've talked about is raising your stupid perfect family on this stupid perfect land. Well, guess what? I'm damaged goods—about as far from perfect as a woman can get."

Without saying another word, he crossed to her, pulling her into his arms. And then he was crying, too. Holding her, rocking her until the last of the sun's rays gave way to the rising moon. With his strong hands, he held her face, kissing her nose and closed eyelids, her forehead and the apples of her cheeks.

"All this time," he said, his voice hoarse from emotion, "I thought it was me. I thought I'd done something to ruin what we had."

"Never." She vehemently shook her head. "You were my world. When you left, I died inside."

"Don't you see? I was dying, too. Hell, I've been walking around half-dead for years without you. Why, *why* didn't you tell me?"

"I'm sorry." And she deeply was.

His next kiss was to her lips, and so sweet, so agonizingly slow and special and heady, that her eyes welled all over again. When he nuzzled her neck, she groaned, arching her head back to allow him space to move his lips to the base of her throat.

When he unbuttoned her blouse, she returned the favor. With their shirts removed and her bra off, he held her that much closer, and the sensation of finally, after all these years, once again feeling him pressed to her, skin to skin, soul to soul, left her dizzy and punch-drunk on raw sensation. Her breasts swelled and her nipples hardened at the sheer excitement of brushing against his coarse chest hair.

Belt buckles and jeans and his boxers and her panties and straw hat were next to go into a pile on the hard-packed ground.

He kept his hat on, and she liked it.

Their kisses turned frantic, deeper, with bold sweeps of their tongues.

His erection pulsed against her and she'd grown wet for him. When he lifted her, only to ease her onto him, she bit his shoulder to keep from crying out in pleasure. When he'd filled her, then established a slow and easy rhythm, she could have wept from joy. Until this moment, she hadn't realized how desperately she'd missed him, needed him, craved him.

"You're so beautiful," he whispered, the words ragged. "I've missed you so bad."

"I—I missed you, too…"

In and out he thrust with her clinging to him, relishing his every move. With the stars above and land he loved so solid below, she felt transported back in time. They could have been teens again, so frantic to taste the forbidden they didn't have patience for flowery romance or foreplay. All they'd needed was this fevered connection to prove their bodies were as united as their souls.

All too soon, she climaxed with an explosion of heat and light behind her closed eyes. When he tensed, then delivered a few more urgent thrusts, he kissed her with what she could only describe as an air of desperation, as if he couldn't get enough of the unspoken bond the two had always shared.

"Wow…" He finally said, resting his forehead against hers. "Wasn't expecting that."

She pressed her lips to his, then asked, "Complaining?"

"Not a bit. But now what?"

"You mean long-term, or the fact that we're both buck naked in a pasture, and I think Misty and Fred are staring?"

"A little of both. But for now—" he set her to her feet "—let's do a little skinny-dipping, then you can cook me that stew."

"Thought you weren't hungry?"

"I lied. If I weren't so damned stubborn, I'd have loved to finish your tasty lunch." He finally removed his hat, flinging it to a bench on their way to the stream's naturally formed swimming hole.

The water was too cold to linger, so after some splashing and a quick rinse, they dressed. Grady lit a fire—the recent storm made finding firewood a breeze, considering how many limbs were down—and while he put up the tent and unrolled cushy pads and their sleeping bags, Jessie started dinner.

With the stew simmering, she sat on the nearest log, watching Grady wrestle with putting on a new lantern mantle by firelight. That morning, if someone had told her that by nightfall her long-held secret would not only be out, but that she and Grady would make love, she'd have called them crazy to their face.

"Got it," he said, then lit the lantern, hanging it from a rod that had long ago been hammered into a tree. "That's better. Now I can see you."

"I'm not sure if I want you to."

"What's that mean?"

"Only that I'm a teacher. We're not exactly known for having sex in the middle of fields."

"Whatever." He stretched out his long legs, touching his boot tips to the rocks circling the fire. He looked so handsome in profile that she had to look away. His strong, stubble-covered jaw and Roman nose and crew-cut hair sporting a wicked case of hat-head all served as a reminder of why she'd never been able to find another man. But just because they'd made love didn't mean they were once again *in* love.

"Sorry. Guess I shouldn't have let things get so carried away. Hell, I didn't even use a condom."

"I don't even know what to say to that. You're *sorry*?"

"You know what I mean." He pulled his legs back and straightened. "I never meant for that to happen. You opened yourself up to me and were vulnerable, and I took advantage."

"Just hush."

"No, I mean it. You've got a problem, and instead of supporting you, I stripped you."

"Grow up, Grady. We *stripped* each other." She moved to stir the stew before she used her wooden spoon to thump the cowboy on his no-good head. "And yes, I do have a problem, but since we're not together, no worries—it doesn't concern you."

"That's not what I meant and you know it. Look…" He stood behind her, easing his arms around her waist. She wanted so badly to lean against him, to absorb his strength, but what was the point? If they fought even after the beautiful act they'd just shared, there was no hope of them ever reuniting. "You're mixing up my words. I'm not sorry because I for one second regret our being together, but because you deserve better than a quick screw in a field."

Jessie gaped, then struggled free from his hold. "Just

when I think you can't offend me more, you go ahead and open your big fat mouth. I told you about my infertility issue because you're right—you do deserve a reason for why I called off our engagement. I didn't tell you because I was looking for a pity lay. Silly me, I thought what just happened—our reconnecting—could be an incredible start to what might be a second chance, but now I see it for what it was. A mistake."

"*Jess*…please don't be like this. You're acting all defensive, and I get that—what you've been through has to have been hard. But I'm not the enemy. I cared about you then, and still do now."

"Great, but what does that even mean? Now that you know the truth, what difference does it really make?"

"Well…" He was back, this time facing her, skimming his fingertips across the crown of her head. "For starters, I fail to see what's keeping us apart." He kissed her, and despite her best intentions, his merest touch ignited a slow burn she felt helpless to douse.

She forced herself to listen to the voice of reason telling her to once again back away. But with him this close, she wasn't strong enough to resist. He smelled of leather and sweat and springtime.

"You know you want to kiss me."

"No." In reality, of course, she did. But as a teacher, discipline played a major role in her life. Since signing her first year's teaching contract, order and restraint had guided her daily moves. Just because she stood in front of her old high school sweetheart, who'd grown into the man of her dreams, didn't give her permission to lose herself to moonlight or his spell. "Why would I want to kiss you when you're leaving next week?"

"What if I asked for more leave? Mom and Dad's insurance money hasn't even come in, and when it does, they're going to need my help. My CO will understand."

"Okay, but even if you stay an extra month or two, what then? It's not like you're going to retire early from the Navy to live here—and even if you did, what difference would it make to the two of us? I'll still be infertile, and you'll still want that perfect family I can never give."

Unable to look at him a moment longer, she used the oven mitt she'd packed to remove the stew from the fire. She lifted the heavy, cast-iron lid, intending to give their meal another stir, but the fire must have been too hot, as the stew had already burned into a black mass so thick her spoon couldn't pass through.

"Great…" Beyond frustrated by the entire night, she flung the pot, spoon and then mitt into the tall grass beyond the lantern and fire's glow. "Just once, why can't anything go right?"

"Maybe because you're so tightly wound you won't let it?"

He fished a couple of muffins from her knapsack and handed her one. "I'm right here, Jess. And for the time being, I'm not going anywhere. Would it kill you to just take a deep breath and jump? To not think about next year or next month, but the next five minutes?"

The notion was tempting.

But what happened when she opened her heart to him all over again—which she inevitably would—and then the finality of her diagnosis fully sank in? He'd leave her. Oh, he wouldn't do it to be cruel. She had no doubt he held feelings for her. But that wouldn't be enough to ultimately sustain a relationship.

"Five minutes…" He skimmed his palms along her upper arms. His heat caused her to shiver. "That's all

I'm asking. And then five minutes after that, if you still want nothing to do with me? Hell, I'll sleep on one of these benches and you can have the whole tent to yourself. Sound good?"

"Yes." *No.* Being apart from him for even a few minutes wasn't in any way what she wanted, but what had to be.

GRADY WOKE SLOWLY to a crook in his neck, and a woman with the nastiest hot breath he'd ever had the misfortune to smell. He cautiously opened his eyes, disbelieving that his Jessie might be the cause of this God-awful funk, only to encounter a tongue wider than his hand. "Misty, what the hell?"

He bolted upright to find the horse nuzzling his forehead.

"Thank you, darlin'—" he rubbed her cheek "—love you, too, but I don't need kisses this morning."

Sometime in the night, Jessie must have covered him where he'd crashed on the bench nearest the fire, as his unzipped, open sleeping bag was coated with dew.

A glance at the tent showed that it was no longer there—neatly folded and placed back in its canvas bag, with Jessie's sleeping bag and both pads rolled alongside it.

Where was she? "Jess?"

He stood, holding his hand to his forehead to protect his eyes from the rising sun. A distant whip-poor-will called from the small lake the brook fed into.

Jessie sat on a boulder alongside the gurgling water, braiding her hair. Her golden waves shone in the sun.

"I like it better down." His boot steps left trails as he walked to her through silvery dew.

"Duly noted." She kept right on braiding until reaching the end, then fastened it with an elastic holder.

He perched next to her. "Truce?"

"I suppose."

"That's encouraging." He nudged her upper arm with his. "Look at me."

"I can't."

"Why?"

"Hurts." Her eyes welled with tears.

Exhausted, not just from his night sleeping on a log bench, but from fighting with her, fighting his feelings for her, he sighed, resting his head on her shoulder.

"Please don't."

He refused to budge. "Don't what? Touch you?"

"Please don't set me up only to let me fall."

"I would never do that. I respect you too much."

"If that's true, then we can't let what happened last night ever happen again. As amazing as it was, it only reminded me how much you used to mean to me. I can't fall for you all over again only to lose you."

"But—" He started to protest, but she put her fingers over his lips.

"If you want a truce for the remainder of your stay, I need your promise—no more touching, no more kissing. Especially, no more…" As her words trailed off, he looked up just in time to see her cheeks blaze. "Well, you know."

"Are you sure? Because I kind of liked the *you-know* portion of our evening."

"Grady…"

"All right, all right." He held out his hand for her to shake. "I'll agree to your terms, but for the record, only because after my rough night's sleep, you've put me under duress."

"Uh-huh…" Her smile killed him. The way it shone all the way from her bow lips to her chocolate-brown eyes. "You're a Navy SEAL. I'm betting you've slept in way worse places."

"Guess you've got me there." He answered her smile with one of his own. "There was this one night in Afghanistan when we thought we were only out for a day's reconnaissance. Turns out our targets were on the move, and by the time we tracked them down, the elevation was high enough for it to be snowing. We spent the night huddled in a freaking cave. Our MREs were long gone, and all we had to eat were a couple cans of Beanie Weenies. One of the guys kept farting, and my pals Wiley and Rowdy and I chose to just sleep outside. It was so cold, I'm surprised I still have ears."

She took one look at him and burst out laughing. "You slept in the snow because some guy passed gas? TMI!"

"You think me getting frostbite's funny?" He happened to know where she was most ticklish and leaned in for the kill.

"No!" she shrieked, laughing while valiantly trying to fend off his attack. "Stop!"

"Not until you tell me you're sorry for laughing at my frostbite."

"Sorry," she managed despite being seized by a fit of laughing tears.

"Thank you." He stopped, but couldn't help but notice how he'd landed on top of her. Her breasts pressed against his chest, causing a whole new commotion beneath his fly. His mouth was mere inches from hers—

close enough for him to smell her hauntingly familiar breath.

"I'm going to break my promise," he warned.

"Please don't." Her breathing quickened and her pupils widened with arousal.

She wanted him. He wanted her.

He failed to see the problem.

"I meant what I said, Grady. I can't handle losing you all over again."

"And if I promise you won't?"

"I wouldn't believe you."

Chapter Ten

"Is that a hickey?" In the kitchen early that evening, prepping for her world-famous chicken-fried steak, Billy Sue inspected Jessie's neck.

"Mom!" Beyond mortified and mad at Grady all over again, Jessie raised the collar on her blue-and-white polka-dotted blouse. He'd given her a hickey? Their encounter had been so wild and shamefully exhilarating, she wasn't all that surprised.

For the rest of the roundup, he'd kept his promise by keeping his hands and lips to himself. They'd found all the missing cattle, unsaddled, brushed the horses and made the short drive back to her parents' all without further incident. She should have been happy that he'd followed her rules, but nothing could be further from the truth.

Too many times to count, she'd caught sight of him when he'd thought she hadn't been looking. When riding through scrub brush, he'd strapped on well-worn leather chaps and, God help her, he'd looked so damned sexy she'd come darn close to breaking her own rules. The way his faded Wranglers hugged his behind ought to be illegal!

"I take it you two had a nice trip?" her mom asked.

"It was all right." Jessie stood at the open fridge, not so much hungry as in need of cooling off. "I burned the stew."

"Oh, no. You must both be starving."

"True," Grady said. He'd been unloading their gear. Jessie had offered to help, but he'd turned her down. She probably should have insisted, but the longer she remained in his proximity, the more she wanted to run her hands up under his shirt and across his rock-hard chest. "Your daughter's an awful cook, and I'm not sure your poor Dutch oven's ever coming clean." He set it on the counter.

Jessie cringed when her mom lifted the heavy lid for a peek inside. "You weren't kidding. This is a mess."

"Told you." Grady took the pot to the sink, filled it with water then set it on the stove. "I'll try boiling this thing clean."

"Thank you," Billy Sue said before dragging her daughter to the pantry, where she traded her pleasant smile for a scowl. "What in the world were you doing that you let my poor pot get so burned? It belonged to your great-great-grandma Edith. It was her sole possession that survived her covered wagon crashing during the great land run—bless her heart. Right about now, I'll bet she's turning in her grave."

"I swear you make that story more tragic every time it's told."

"Don't you sass me, Jessie Anne. I'm sure Edith didn't tolerate that nonsense, either—especially from a girl sporting a you-know-what."

Jessie closed her eyes.

Now would have been a fine time for lightning to strike her, not necessarily dead, but crispy enough to warrant an ER visit and thus an escape from her crazy mother. She forced a few deep breaths before summoning the courage to ask, "How did your TV appearance go? Did you find Angel's parents?"

"As a matter of fact, no. She's napping upstairs." Billy Sue nodded toward the baby monitor resting on the counter alongside the cookie jar. "The whole city council's baffled."

"I'll bet." Was it wrong that Jessie's shoulders sagged in secret relief that she'd at least get to see Angel one more time? "Need help with dinner?"

"Thanks, but I'm just about done. Why don't you get cleaned up? You smell like horse—and be sure to cover that hickey. Grady's mom isn't as progressive as me."

On that note, Jessie left the pantry.

"Look!" Grady stood at the stove, wielding a meat fork with a giant black mass attached. "I got the stew to come out. No, all this pot needs is a little elbow grease and it'll be good as new."

Cotton barked at the black mass.

"Thank you," Billy Sue hugged Grady from behind. "Great-Great-Grandma Edith would be proud. You're such a good boy."

"Suck-up," Jessie mumbled on her way up the stairs. Nice how her mom had conveniently forgotten who'd given her that stupid hickey!

GRADY WAS RELIEVED to be reunited with his and Jessie's families—not because he'd particularly missed them, but their presence made it easier to abide by the no-touching-or-kissing promise he'd made to Jessie.

Once again, the six of them—seven, counting Angel—were seated poolside for dinner. Roger had lit tiki torches and spring peepers provided bonus ambience. Grady sat across from Jessie and once again regretted that promise. Every time he looked up, there she was, unwittingly teasing him in her pretty blue sundress that showed off her bare shoulders but had a collar high enough to hide the unfortunate souvenir of their union that he'd never meant to leave behind. Even better—or worse, considering he could look all he wanted but wasn't allowed to touch—she'd worn her long hair just the way he liked, all loose and wavy.

Angel cried in her carrier and Jessie reached her first.

Since Jessie had told him about her condition, Grady hadn't given it much thought. The notion that she couldn't have babies didn't compute. In his line of work, he saw problems and fixed them. Period.

In his world, the word *impossible* didn't exist.

Since he was big on planning, what he was thinking was that he'd do a little wooing to get Jessie back in his court. Maybe take her out to a nice dinner or two. A picnic here and there. Once he got her to drop her ridiculous notion that the two of them shouldn't kiss, it would that much easier to get down to the business of once again making her his.

Already in a better mental place, he dug into the delicious meal. "Billy Sue, you are one heck of a cook."

Jessie's mom beamed. "Why, thank you, sweetheart."

Everyone else agreed.

He glanced at Jessie to find her moving her food around. Had she taken his compliment to her mom as a dig about her disastrous stew?

"Jess," he said, "one of these days I'd love trying your stew again. I can't tell you how many meals I've annihilated over a campfire."

"Really?" Gaze dangerously narrowed, she cocked her head. "Because the way I remember it, the only reason my *delicious* stew burned was because of your big, fat mouth."

"Jessie Anne!" Billy Sue scowled at her daughter. "Talk like that makes you sound more like one of your students than their teacher."

"Oh, dear…" Rose pat Jessie's back. "Grady, what did you do?"

"Me? Nothing." He kept shoveling food into his mouth. This was hardly the appropriate time to rehash what had actually caused dinner to burn—the mother of all fights that, looking back on it, he deeply regretted.

Dinner finally came to an end, and after helping Roger and his dad clean up—more to avoid Jessie than because he was a good guy—Grady finally went upstairs, only to find her bathing Angel.

His breath caught in his throat.

Jessie had knelt beside the tub and was softly singing, "Row, row, row your boat, gently down the stream…"

Angel reclined in her pink baby-bath lounger while Jessie applied no-tear shampoo to her hair.

Chest tight, Grady approached slowly.

"Is she smiling?" He knelt alongside Jessie.

"Sure looks like it, doesn't it? If this is her first grin, I feel awful that her parents aren't here to see."

"No kidding." He touched his pinkie finger to the palm of Angel's tiny hand, and when she took hold with a surprisingly strong grip he couldn't stop grinning. "Don't tell any of my guys, but, Lord, I love babies. They have this way of putting everything in perspective, you know?"

She nodded, but when her eyes filled with tears yet again, he knew he'd said the wrong thing.

"Look…" Until something could be done about Jessie's condition, he owed it to her to knock it off with the baby talk. "I was going to wait to bring this up, but while we were riding this afternoon, I had a lot of time to think. Not to get into your private business, but on your baby thing, have you gotten a second opinion?"

He rocked back on his heels, fully prepared for another round of sparring, but all she did was nod. "Try four or five. The disease I have caused scarring in my fallopian tubes. I'm lucky, in that I don't have the severe pain many women do, but my reproductive organs are a mess."

"But that can be fixed, right?"

"This isn't like crossing a rain-swollen river. The reproductive system is a little more complex." Lips pressed tight, she took a plastic cup from the tub's edge to use for rinsing Angel's curls.

"Please don't think for a second that I'm trying to downplay the situation. I just want to help."

"I understand. And appreciate that. What you don't know—what my busybody mother doesn't even know—is that last year over summer break, I had a procedure to hopefully clear away some of the worst of the scarring. Since the scarring will only get heavier with age, I opted to try in vitro fertilization. Long story short, after three tries, it still didn't take, so I tossed in the proverbial towel. I was crushed. And tired. And for whatever reason, I figured it just wasn't meant to be." She sniffed back tears, and when he clasped her hand beneath the tub's warm water she didn't protest. "Now, with my students, I have a never-ending supply of smiling faces and, aside from sometimes being lonely, I'm okay. I've accepted the inevitable and moved on with my life. If you still have any affection left for me at all, I'm begging you to please drop the subject and leave me alone."

What if I can't?

Angel gurgled, and when she raised her hand, then let it fall to slap the water, she smiled again before making even more splashes.

"You're adorable," Jessie whispered to the baby.

"What about me?" Grady asked, hoping to lend levity to the situation.

"You have your moments—unfortunately, they're few and far between." She winked.

JESSIE HAD AN impossible time falling asleep, which was why she now sat in the rocker in Angel's nursery with her knees hugged to her chest.

If it weren't so late, she would have called her friend Corny. Her nickname might be silly, but she usually gave great advice. But then what good was that when Jessie was so confused by Grady's reentry into her life that she wouldn't even know what questions to ask?

She'd thought the whole fertility issue was behind her. She'd accepted it as fact and moved on—she'd done the same with Grady being out of her life. But now that he was back—even if only temporarily—her mind and heart felt all mixed-up. In under two weeks, she'd lost her home and the school where she worked, and now the belief that she'd be okay living the rest of her life without a husband or child.

Which was kind of crazy.

She'd supported herself for years. She was independent and happy. But if that were entirely true, then why was she looking at Angel and wondering how in the world she'd ever let her go?

"What are you doing up so late?" Wearing only boxers, Grady entered the room, stopping in front of Angel's crib. "Don't you have work in the morning?"

"Yeah. We're getting the church nursery school set up for classes. The principal wants us open for business by Wednesday."

"Think that's enough time?"

"Nowhere close, but it's not as if the boss gave me a vote."

"I know the feeling. Need help assembling your new room?"

No. The last thing I need is to be around you one second more. Instead of listening to her head, Jessie's confused heart said, "Thanks. That would be nice."

She pushed herself up from the rocker, hyperaware of Grady—and how little he wore. Before her apartment had been obliterated, she'd never felt overly exposed in a tank and boy shorts, but now she remembered all too clearly how intoxicating it had felt having him against her, inside her, and her skin turned superheated and her cheeks flushed. Every inch of her craved going to him for just a simple hug. That was all. Then she'd be a good girl and turn away.

Oh, who was she fooling?

With any luck, that hug would lead to stroking and caressing and— She crossed her arms to cover her suddenly puckered nipples.

"I'm, uh, headed to bed. See you in the morning." Judging by the bulge in his boxers, he had difficulties of his own.

"Sweet dreams." The words were easy enough to say,

but her current thoughts were anything but sweet. She had never wanted Grady more. And she'd never been more acutely aware of the fact that no matter what, she couldn't have him.

At 5:00 a.m., Grady woke with wood—just like when he'd finally drifted off to sleep. Knowing his ultimate release slept in the room next door didn't make his untenable situation any easier.

He took care of business in the shower, then dressed in camo fatigues and a Virginia is For Lovers T-shirt.

He was headed downstairs when he heard Angel crying.

"Hey, gorgeous. Why are you up so early?" He lifted her from the crib to cuddle her to his chest. The simple act of holding her wreathed him in her heady baby scent. Pink lotion and tearless shampoo. An unidentifiable something sweet that compelled him to want a half-dozen babies all his own.

She made a gurgling sound, then burrowed closer.

"Hungry? I make a mean bottle."

In the kitchen, he could have set her in her carrier, but preferred holding her for as long as he had the chance. It couldn't be much longer now till her parents were found.

He filled a saucepan with hot tap water, then opened a fresh can of formula. He made the bottle, then popped it in the pan to warm.

"Last summer, my good friends Cooper and Millie had a baby. Coop used to be a SEAL, but he quit the Navy to run his ranch. He's also got a pretty awesome camp, where he trains civilians to get SEAL tough. Maybe one day you could go there with your folks."

Her grin did funny things to his stomach.

"You're going to be a heartbreaker, aren't you?"

She gifted him with a baby giggle.

He took her bottle from the water and shook a few drops of formula on the underside of his wrist. "Feels good."

In the family room, he sat on the sofa, cradling her to put the bottle to her lips. Feeding Angel made his mind drift to Jessie's confession. He understood why her fear of not having kids drove her to break things off with him, but what if that fear was unfounded?

Even if it turned out to be true, why had she taken away his right to choose? What didn't she understand about the fact that, more than anything, he just wanted to spend the rest of his life with her? Once they were officially back on the same page, they could fix the whole kid thing. Until then, all that mattered was getting together—and *staying* together.

Chapter Eleven

"Thank you for meeting me." Jessie slid into the booth at Cecil's Diner opposite her friend Cornelia. Jessie was due at the church where they'd be setting up her temporary classroom, but not for an hour. Cecil's was one of only three restaurants that had survived the storm, and was already packed to capacity with a line out the front door. Patsy Cline played on the jukebox and the comfort-food scents of syrup and bacon made Jessie's stomach growl. "I'm a wreck."

"*You're* a wreck?" Corny added cream and four sugars to her coffee. "Our house was saved—which is fantastic—but we've got two families living with us who weren't so lucky, and since there's no school till Wednesday, that means seven bored kids going bonkers."

Seven kids, and here she couldn't even have one. Jessie tried focusing on her friend's legitimate woes, but felt too wrapped up in her own pain to help.

"...so then Alicia decided to use real eggs, bacon and OJ in Felicity's play kitchen. It took three of us moms an hour to clean and sanitize it."

"That's awful, and I don't mean to sound insensitive, but I've got a real emergency here. Grady and I..." Jessie couldn't even bring herself to say *made love* out loud.

Because really, what happened between them had been more like straight-up sex.

"Shut the front door." Corny set down her coffee and stared. "Are you back together?"

"No. Of course not. And before I go any further, I'm still ticked at you and Allen for seeing Grady when he was in town without even telling me."

"Sorry, but he specifically asked Allen to be sure we kept you away."

"Kept me away? As though I meant nothing more to him than a dread disease?" Jessie covered her face with her hands.

The waitress dropped off coffee for her, and took their orders for pancakes and bacon.

"It wasn't like that at all," Corny said. "Allen got the feeling that it was more a case of Grady being afraid to see you—as if it would hurt."

Was that any better? Jessie groaned. "This is all such a mess. So we were together, and it was the hottest, naughtiest, down-and-dirty encounter of my life."

"*Holy crap!* Details!" Corny leaned closer. "I'm talking specifics. Allen and I are in a dry spell, and—"

"I'm not telling you anything beyond what I already have—which was too much. Suffice to say, now that my body knows what it's been missing, it craves more. My head knows better, and my heart is somewhere in between."

"Holy smokes…" Corny fanned herself with one of the plastic menus stashed behind the napkin holder. "Last time Grady was over, he and Allen played football with Al Jr. in the backyard. All the guys took their shirts off and Grady was a sight to behold. Those abs…"

Her far-off, dreamy expression perfectly summed up Jessie's feelings.

"I know, right? Being pressed against him was like touching—" She stopped herself before going further. "No. I can't dwell on this a second longer."

"Agreed." Corny added more sugar to her coffee. "But what are you going to do? Allen said Grady is now on extended leave until his folks get back on their feet. With him around, how are you planning not to fall for him all over again? Assuming you haven't already?"

Jessie's stomach clenched.

"Oh, dear… You did, didn't you? You're as hot for him as ever, but the whole infertility issue is still between you. Did you tell him?"

"Everything. But then he came back with this Mr. Fix-It attitude, as if with one wave of his magic SEAL wand, everything would be better. I told him about my surgery and the IVF. I made it very clear that barring a full-on miracle, multiple doctors have told me I would most likely never conceive."

"Okay, but how is he with adoption? You guys have been watching the mystery baby, right? Doesn't she make it easy to see how biology doesn't have to be a factor when falling for a child in need of a home?"

"All too easy. But that's the problem—sooner or later, her family will be found. Then what? Last thing I want is for Grady and I to fall back in love, only to end up right where we started."

"Would that be so bad—the love part?"

"Yes. Because I get the impression that he believes my infertility is an issue he can bulldoze through. As if with enough brute strength, he could will me pregnant—if we were even back together. Which we're not."

"Hmm…" Corny added more cream to her coffee. "You have to love that take-charge quality, though. I can't count the number of guys you've thought you might have a relationship with who've bolted when you tell them up front about your condition. Yet here's Grady, already willing to fight."

"I know, but that's just it—he's all gung-ho now, but what happens if we do get together, but then he realizes my doctors were right and he was wrong? He seriously wants a whole herd of his *own* kids. When he finally accepts he'll never have them with me, I know he'll feel bad about it, but he'll realize there's nothing he can do but move on."

The waitress delivered their food.

Never had Jessie been more in need of butter, warm syrup and bacon.

"That's your own fears and insecurities talking. What if just the opposite happens, and he realizes how much he loves you and never wants to let you go?"

Jessie snorted. "Are you on a sugar high? I long ago accepted the fact that fairy tales don't come true for women like me. Case in point—my house just blew away, and I didn't land in Oz, but at my crazy mother's."

THE LAST TIME Grady stepped foot in a church, he'd been deep undercover in Croatia. The Cathedral of St. James had taken nearly a hundred years to build, and hadn't been completed until 1535. Terrorists had planted a bomb in it, and if they'd had their way, the UNESCO World Heritage Site would have been rubble.

Grady's team found the bomb in time, then rounded up the bad guys, delivering them to the proper authorities, who ensured they'd be locked up for a nice, long while.

The sense of awe he'd felt in the cathedral's hallowed space had filled him with not only wonder, but resolution to do whatever it took to help his team get their job done.

The church he now stood in might not be anywhere near as grand as that cathedral, but his determination to win back Jessie, and for them to go on to have the family they'd always dreamed of, was just as strong.

In the church's Sunday-school wing, he wandered down a long central corridor, checking in each room, until finally finding Jessie in what the label on the door declared to be the Kindergarten-Kave. "Hey, gorgeous."

"Hey. You found me."

He winced. "Considering this is the only church within the city limits still standing, it wasn't too hard."

"True." As if on edge, she shifted her weight from one foot to the other, and held her hands clasped tight at her midsection. None of that had any bearing on the fact that even in her work clothes of khaki shorts and a T-shirt, with her hair more down than up in a messy bun, she still held the power to steal his breath. She forced a smile. "My students are going to have a fit when they see this room was meant for kids younger than them. At least most of the desks survived. The principal, PE teacher and a few homeroom dads have been washing muck off them all day. They've delivered them to the back door. Would you mind helping me carry my allotted eighteen?"

"No problem—but if you've got other things to do in here, I don't mind hauling them myself."

"Thanks. That would be great."

The task took about ten minutes.

Back in the room, he clumped the desks into the three groups of six she'd requested. Then he stood there like an idiot—feeling like a Clydesdale in a minefield. He might be great with babies, but in here, all the chair backs came up to his knees, and Jessie sat at her desk, meticulously cutting what he guessed were bulletin board letters out of paper.

Feeling antsy, he asked, "What do you need me to do next?"

"Let me finish these last few letters, and then if you don't mind, I'll need help assembling my welcome-back board."

"Last time I snipped bomb leads, I was a pretty good cutter."

She stopped working her scissors to shake her head and smile. "If you think you can do it, be my guest." She shoved a pile of construction-paper letters needing to be cut across her desk in his direction.

"Oh—I know I can do it." He snatched kid scissors from a green plastic tub, then sat on the reading-corner table to get down to work—only his fingers didn't fit in the holes. He raised his hand. "Teacher?"

Yes. He'd earned another grin.

"Thought you said you had this job tackled?"

"I did—would—but I'm gonna need big-boy scissors."

She put down her own work in progress to fish through her top drawer. "Will these work?"

"Much better. Thanks." He transformed from mere mortal into a cutting machine. Competition brought out the best in him, and this situation was as good as any to prove his cutting prowess.

"Watch those corners, mister. Neatness counts."

"What do you mean? These are awesome." He glanced at his efforts and was crushed by her lack of approval.

She left her chair and now leaned close enough for him to pick up the sweet strawberry scent of her shampoo.

"Like this…" She wrapped her hand around his, killing him by violating her own no-touching rule—not that he was complaining. But when her soft curls brushed his cheek, he held his breath to keep from closing the short distance needed to kiss her.

How was this not affecting her like it was him? His heartbeat had turned erratic, and every inch of him hummed with awareness.

"See what I mean?" She glanced his way, tucking her hair behind her ear with her free hand. Then their gazes locked. As if just now realizing her hand still rested atop his, she backed away. "But if you want, I can handle the rest."

"I'm good."

For the next twenty minutes, they cut the remaining letters in silence. What was she thinking? Had she been surprised by their chemistry even in a church? She shouldn't be. That elemental attraction between them was the reason they'd both remained single all these years. She could deny it all she wanted, but they were made for each other.

"Done." He held up his last letter.

"Awesome. Thanks." She nodded to the bulletin board just to the right of the entry. "I already hung the background paper, but I made a rainbow that's going to be a two-man job to staple."

"I'm on it." And he was. But he hadn't expected a simple staple job to turn into a complex game of Twister.

While hanging the flimsy paper, their arms and legs brushed, causing him all kinds of physical and emotional distress. Had he known helping her would be this much of a struggle, he'd have stayed home watching Westerns with his dad, who'd strained his back clearing debris.

"Whew," she said when they were finally done. "I didn't think that rainbow would be so hard. Now we just have to put up the letters."

"You know—" he hitched his thumb toward the door "—since you're the letter expert, I'm going to head outside to see if the guys need more help moving desks."

"Oh. Okay." Her expression read crestfallen, and he was sorry about that, but he needed a time-out. The woman had him more hot and bothered than she had on prom night—no doubt because back then, after she'd spent hours torturing him on the dance floor, he'd at least known that once they escaped their friends, the odds of him getting lucky had pretty much been a sure thing.

Now? He was hot and bothered and dangerously close to sporting wood in a church-turned-school. Not good.

Still pouty, she asked, "Want to meet later for lunch? I made sandwiches."

"I appreciate the offer, but should probably check on Dad. While you were at breakfast with Corny, he went to the ranch without me, then wrestled with a tractor tire and lost." Inwardly, Grady groaned. Of course, he wanted share breakfast, lunch and dinner with Jessie, but he was unprepared for how deeply the mere act of being in her presence messed with his head.

"Oh, no. Is he going to be okay?"

"I'm sure. Mom's with Billy Sue at the day care. At one, they're taking Angel to the police station. A couple called from Seattle who said they still have family missing who may have been caught in the storm."

"You're just now telling me this?" She tossed her remaining few loose letters to a student desk while taking her purse from a drawer in her own desk.

"What are you doing?"

"What do you think? Going to the police station. What if these people aren't legit and they try taking Angel without proper documentation? I couldn't live with myself, knowing she was illegally snatched."

"Jess, stop." She'd almost reached the door when he cut her off at the pass. "Police aren't going to let just anyone take her."

Tears filled her eyes.

Screw her rules.

Grady pulled Jessie into his arms, and she let him. "We knew all along this day was coming. Let's both go to the police station, and hopefully we'll at least get to say goodbye."

"What if I can't?" she asked, her words muffled against his chest.

"Let's take this one step at a time, starting with looking on the bright side. Remember how despondent Angel was when we first got her? Think how happy she'll be to get back with her family. Would you deny her that joy?"

She shook her head.

"Okay, so let's drive over together—and bring your sandwiches. I'm sure they're delicious, and we'll eat them on the way."

"Yes." Her lone word sounded as faint as if she'd spoken through fog. "I'll grab the sandwiches. Only I'm not very hungry."

"That's all right. I'll eat both."

He released her long enough to take her soft-sided lunch cooler from where she'd hooked it over her chair, then was back beside her, guiding her out of the building and into his car.

She moved as if in a trance, and that scared him.

He hadn't realized how close she'd grown to Angel, but then what was he saying? He was more than a little fond of the cutie himself.

"When we get there?" she asked, keeping a white-knuckled grip on her purse. "Will you stay with me—no matter what?"

"There's nowhere I'd rather be." He took her hand, easing his fingers between hers.

"I'm trying to be strong—I've steeled myself to be ready for this, but now that the time to give Angel back to her family might really be here, I selfishly don't want to let her go. For just a little while, like when we had her in the tub last night—" she sniffed "—it was all too easy to pretend she was ours."

Is that what you want? His pulse raced at what may have been an accidental confession.

"I think this is happening now—so soon after, well, you know—to remind me that no matter how badly I want to be a mother, it just isn't meant to be."

"Please don't think I'm trying to be cruel." He tightened his grip on the wheel while zigzagging through debris. "But if I hear you say a crap thing like that one more time, I'm gonna hit something. Did you ever stop to think that you're destined to be a great mother no matter how it happens? You act as if natural childbirth is the only way to have kids, but there are probably thousands—hell, millions—of kids out there searching for homes, which you are well suited to provide, yet you've got this whiny broken record playing in your head that's stuck on the same defeated song."

"Shut up, Grady. You don't understand."

"You're right." He veered into the police-station lot, and parked next to her mom's car. "I don't understand how a woman as smart as you can sometimes act so freaking dumb."

Chapter Twelve

Jessie was so stunned by Grady's accusation that it took her a few seconds to even process his words. How dare he accuse her of being dumb, when he was the one always spouting off about how much he wanted his own, *blood-related* children?

As soon as he parked the car, she hopped out, practically sprinting to the station's door in her haste to escape him.

Allen manned the front desk. "You guys are just in time. The folks who came to claim the baby are in the break room with both of your moms."

"Thanks, man." The guys shook hands.

Jessie was still so miffed with Grady she couldn't stand looking at him. *Maybe because you know he's right?*

The maddening thing about the question she'd asked herself was that part of her feared it was true. She was in such a panic over Angel's family being found, because the time she'd spent with her proved how easy it was to fall for any child. Of course, the notion of bonding for nine months and feeling her baby's first kick and breastfeeding were her idea of bliss—so much so that she'd adopted an all-or-nothing mentality in regard to her infertility issue. If she couldn't have her own baby, she didn't want one at all. But if that was the case, then why had she blamed her unhappiness on Grady, when all he'd tried to do since she'd told him was help?

In the break room, Jessie stood with her back pressed against the counter that held the coffee machine, microwave, sink and three boxes of assorted doughnuts.

"I'm so nervous." The female half of the couple who'd come to inspect Angel wouldn't stop fussing with her hair. Jessie irrationally hated the stranger for the pain she was about to inflict. "We live in Seattle, and it makes me sad that our family has grown apart to the degree that I didn't even know my cousin was in an accident, let alone that Chrissy died." She made the sign of the cross on her chest.

Was Jessie the only one who found it odd that this woman showed up out of nowhere if she hadn't even been close to her cousin? Something about her set off alarms in Jessie's gut.

The stranger kept talking. "The last time we chatted was Christmas, and I knew she was pregnant, but my kids were tearing the house apart, and I didn't get to ask her how far along. She and Jeremy—that's her husband—lived in Phoenix, so I don't even know what they were doing in Oklahoma."

Hello? No one besides her found any of this strange?

"How did you find out about the accident?" Billy Sue asked the woman, all the while holding Angel to her chest. The A/C in the building was chilly, so she'd swaddled the baby in a pink receiving blanket.

"Through police. Chrissy's parents are both deceased, and her husband, Jeremy's, estranged from his family in New Jersey. I know this must sound odd, that I didn't know my own cousin had her baby, but even though the police said her medical records show she wasn't even pregnant, since she told me otherwise, I had to check."

"Of course," Billy Sue said. "The baby's DNA is on record, so you'll need to be tested before police release the infant to you."

"But we're family. We don't need a test."

The hell you don't! Jessie was about two seconds from losing it.

"So sorry for the inconvenience—" Billy Sue graced her with a warm mayoral smile "—but please understand that for the infant's safety, we need to take all precautions. What was your name again?"

The guy pushed his chair back and stood. "Liz, let's go. I told you this wouldn't work."

His wife, or girlfriend or whatever, began crying. She reached for Angel, but Grady shot between her and Billy Sue.

"Not so fast," he said. "Don't know what kind of scam you're pulling, but why don't you beat it before this gets any more out of hand."

Finally! Someone besides her realized these people were charlatans.

When the couple left without saying another word, relief sagged Jessie's shoulders. They weren't Angel's family after all. Which meant the baby would still be in her life. Was that selfish? Absolutely. Even worse, the fact that for whatever reason this couple had tried stealing a baby smacked of the desperation Jessie had begun feeling inside. Not that she would ever go that far, but it was scary seeing a woman who would.

How thin was the veil separating Jessie from that kind of mental instability?

"Good gracious." Rose cupped her hand to the back of Angel's head. "Just what do you suppose they had planned?"

"Don't know, don't wanna know," Billy Sue said. "Just glad we stopped them before finding out. I had my doubts about those two all along. There was something fishy about their story."

"Agreed," Rose said.

"Ready to get out of here?" Grady whispered in Jessie's ear. His warm breath tickled, and caused her to shiver.

She nodded. "We need to talk."

WE NEED TO TALK.

The most dreaded words in the English language. They said their goodbyes to their moms and Angel, then Grady walked Jessie to his rental.

Behind the wheel with her safely buckled in, he dared ask, "We're alone. What's up?"

"I'm sorry." Focusing her gaze straight ahead, she drew her lower lip into her mouth. "You're right, I have been dumb. Seeing that woman in there—the lengths she was willing to go to for a baby—scared me. Not that I'm emotionally anywhere near where she is, but I understand how a woman gets to that point. All these years, I've been holding this problem inside, but not until just now—when you pretty much told me to wake up—did I see how blessed I am. So what if I can't have my own baby? I'm going to check into adoption—today."

"Jess…" A muscle in his jaw ticked. "I'm glad you're taking a proactive route, but are you sure you're ready? I mean, I'm all for you adopting. It's a great idea. But do you think maybe you should at least wait until you have an address?"

"Are you kidding me? After your big rah, rah, pro-adoption speech, now you're going to backpedal?"

He took her hands, and she surprisingly didn't stop him. "That's not what I'm saying at all. I'm just thinking maybe it would be best for you to get past the stress of having your home blown away before you take on the challenge of raising a child. For now, isn't Angel enough?"

"She would be—*could* be—but you know as well as I do that her family is out there somewhere. I can't trust my heart with her any more than I can trust it with you, Grady. Both of you are temporary fixtures in my life—wonderful, but fleeting."

"What if it didn't have to be that way?" He stroked the tops of her hands with his thumbs.

"What are you saying?" Her gaze searched his.

"I don't know." Lord, he wanted to unbuckle her seat belt, then drag her onto his lap and kiss her till they were both breathing heavy. What *was* he saying? "I guess just that if you wanted, we could start over. Leave the past in the past and start fresh from here."

"How? You live in Virginia, and eventually you'll go back to the Navy."

"What if I didn't—I mean, of course, I'll have to eventually, but I could file for an early discharge." He'd be lying if he said the prospect of not remaining tied to the career he'd worked so hard for didn't scare the hell out of him, but the thought of leaving Jessie just when he'd found her again hurt just as bad. "What if just like we talked about all those years ago, we built a little house on the ranch? Dad already gave me a hundred acres. We could get our own cattle and horses and chickens and—"

"What happened to us starting fresh? Because I know the next thing out of your mouth is going to concern having a kid herd of your own."

"Damn straight. We'll pull a Brad and Angelina and adopt them from all over the globe."

"I want to believe that would work, but wasn't it you who just lectured me about slowing down?"

He laughed. "You got me. All right, so I might be getting a little ahead of myself, but you do that to me. I swear, you're like a virus."

"And that's a good thing?" She wrinkled her adorable nose.

"Very." He kissed her nose, and then her lips. Rules be damned. From here on out he'd touch her whenever he damn well pleased.

When he released her, she looked dazed.

"Where do we go from here?" she asked.

"If you don't mind, I want to check on Dad, but I guess first I should get you back to your temporary school."

"Okay. Sure." Her next look was indecipherable. She'd narrowed her gaze, almost as if asking, "That's it?" Had she expected something more? Like an official proposal? No. He must be reading her all wrong, because it'd only been in the past thirty minutes or so that he'd even been allowed to touch her.

"Twice in one day? I'm flattered." Cornelia held open her front door to let Jessie through.

A big shaggy dog and three kids dashed outside.

"What's up?" Corny asked.

"Sorry to bug you. I know you've got a lot on your plate." Jessie sidestepped the LEGO river flowing across the wooden entry hall floor. From the living room, *Frozen* blared on TV.

"No worries. Let me turn down the movie and we can talk while I cook dinner. Pay me for my counseling services by slicing or dicing something."

"Deal."

After Cornelia assembled all the ingredients necessary for Jessie to make a salad, she started on browning ground beef for cheeseburger-flavored Hamburger Helper. "So what's the latest problem?"

Jessie gave her the Cliff Notes version of the day's events, starting with the unbearable chemistry stemming from bulletin-board assembly to Grady's adoption lecture, to the nut jobs who'd attempted to take Angel.

"Holy crap." Corny gave the meat a stir. "You *have* had a rough day. So out of everything, what's got you most upset?"

"Actually—" she sliced down on a head of red leaf lettuce "—the part seriously bugging me happened after all that. Before heading into the police station, I gave Grady a rough time, but once I absorbed what he was saying, I got it, and then we shared this amazing kiss. He asked if I wanted to start over, and mentioned retiring from the Navy to work the ranch, and I honestly thought he was on the verge of proposing. But that would be crazy, right? I mean, we've only been together barely over a week."

"True." Corny drained the meat. "But if you count all the years you were together in high school, plus the time you've spent pining for him, that adds up to like, what? A decade? If you want to marry him, I'll not only volunteer to be your matron of honor, but bake you a great big cake that says 'finally' on top."

"Did I hear *cake*?" Allen walked in with a kid hanging from each leg. One Jessie recognized as Al Jr., but she'd never seen the other boy.

"Cake! Cake! Cake!" The two cuties chanted.

"Hey, hon." When Cornelia left the stove to kiss her man, a jealous pang tore through Jessie—not that she begrudged her friends their happiness, but she sure would love a big slice of happy pie all her own.

"That was some mess down at the station, huh?" Allen nabbed a slice of green pepper.

"Thank goodness you all had the foresight to run the baby's DNA information."

"Wish I could claim credit, but it's standard procedure."

"No match with any storm victims?" There went her pulse again. Her heart beat so hard, she heard it pounding in her ears.

"Nope. It's crazy. It's as if she literally just fell from the sky."

Jessie summoned her courage to ask, "What happens if no one claims her?"

"Not sure. I would assume she'd go into foster care until someone is found to adopt her. Shoot, as much as your family has taken a liking to her, you might as well toss your hat into the official ring."

"You think so?" Nothing would make her happier. Plus, if she had Angel, would that make Grady all the more likely to stay?

"You totally should," Corny said. "I know you don't like talking about it, but after all you've gone through with the IVF and everything, who knows? Maybe Angel truly is heaven-sent?"

"You guys have no idea how badly I want to believe that, but the scenario of me being able to keep her means she has no family, which makes me the world's most selfish woman."

"I wouldn't go that far..." Corny teased with a wag of her stirring spoon.

Jessie sighed. "All this adoption talk is making me antsy to see her. Guess I should head home."

"Stay," the disgustingly happy couple said in unison.

They next shared a laugh, which left Jessie craving her own soul-deep connection with a man. But who was she fooling? She didn't want just any man but Grady.

"Babe?" Allen had left his wife to rummage in the freezer. "Do we have any more of those sausages your parents brought from Chicago?"

"I think so. Want me to thaw them so you can put them on the grill? I've got a double batch of Hamburger Helper, but that doesn't feel very festive if we're having a party."

"You're not having a party." Jessie tossed the cucumber she'd just chopped onto the salad. "I told you I'm going home."

"Wait." Allen had his phone out. He put it on speaker.

"Hey, man. What's up?" Jessie's pulse galloped merely hearing Grady's voice on the other end of the line.

"Corny and I are having a cookout, and we figured you'd want to come. Dan and Stacy are staying with us. Remember them from school?"

"Sure. Dan used to tell the lamest jokes."

"Yep." Allan laughed. "He still does. Since the storm,

we've got another couple camped with us, too—Nick and Kristi. They're good folks."

"Cool. I look forward to meeting them. Is it all right if I wrangle Jess into coming?"

"Hope so, since she's already here."

For the rest of his conversation, Allen wandered into the living room, with the boys making vrooming race-car sounds while still attached to his legs.

Jessie said, "He seems like a great dad."

"Who? My Allen or your Grady? You do realize you've been starry-eyed ever since Hubby got him on the phone."

"Of course I meant Allen. And as for any looks, I think you must have hamburger grease in your eyes. Grady and I are just exploring our options."

"Uh-huh." Corny added the sauce mix, milk and noodles into her pan. "Which was why you came running over here, thinking he was on the verge of proposing, then being all pouty faced when he didn't?"

"I don't pout." She helped herself to a can opener to work on the black olives. "And I sure don't think there's going to be a wedding any time soon."

An HOUR LATER, when Jessie glanced up from helping Corny, she locked stares with Grady, who happened to be carrying Angel. Jessie's annoying pulse revved to a full-blown canter, yet time itself slowed as if she was living a romantic comedy. How was it possible that after all these years, Grady could still be so handsome he took her breath away? And then there was sweet baby Angel, whose blond curls shone in the golden early-evening sun. The two together made Jessie think crazy things—like what if she really could legally adopt Angel? Even better, what if she and Grady adopted her together—as a married couple?

"Hey." Jessie abandoned her table-setting duties to gravitate toward them—her ready-made family who weren't yet even hers. She kissed Angel's cheek, and in the process, drank in Grady's all-male smell of leather and sweat and that extra something her heart had always recognized as him. "How'd you manage to wrangle this little one away from my mom?"

"Hey, yourself." He reached out as if planning to hug her, but then stopped midway. Her needy body launched a formal protest in the form of an ache in the back of her throat. "Actually, our parents are off on a double date. After an early dinner in Norman, they're all meeting Mom and Dad's contractor at the ranch to go over plans."

"How's your dad's back?"

"Much better since he has a big fat insurance check in hand."

"Wonderful," Jessie said, truly thrilled for Grady's parents. "I'll bet your mom's happy, too."

"She sure is—especially since she's getting a double vanity, whirlpool tub and a dishwasher in the new house."

"Nice. But wait—" Jessie wrinkled her nose. "Your mom's *never* had a dishwasher?"

"Nope. She's old-school about her dishes. Dad talked her into it."

"He deserves a hug. She's going to love all of her new additions."

"For sure."

Their gazes met and locked, and for the longest time she held her breath, not sure what to say or think. The only thing she did know was that she could have stayed like this forever. The three of them, immersed in the backdrop of a happy home with friends laughing in the yard and the mouthwatering scent of sausage cooking on the grill. Toss in her best friend's romantic country playlist and all was ridiculously right with the world.

Only, was it?

Jessie swallowed past the lump in her throat at the realization that this night might as well have been the equivalent of an all-expenses-paid vacation—amazing while it lasted, but the moment she got home, reality, with its loneliness and bills and nights spent with a chick flick and Lean Cuisine, would again be her norm.

"Want to introduce me to Allen and Corny's new housemates?" He left Angel's diaper bag in the entry hall.

"Sure." Jessie ignored the voice inside begging her not to fall any harder for Grady by taking his hand and leading him toward the impromptu party.

"I'll be damned." Dan rose to greet Grady with a back-slapping man hug.

"Language," Dan's wife, Stacy, said before claiming a hug of her own. "Grady Matthews, how'd you go and get even better looking than when you left?"

"Watch it," Dan warned with a good-natured grin. "Everyone knows I'm the biggest hunk in town—which reminds me of a great joke I know you're going to love."

All present laughed and groaned.

"Lay it on me." Grady shifted Angel to his other hip, kissing her forehead in the process.

"All right, so there's this woman who's done so many nice things for people that one day a fairy godmother shows up and grants her three thank-you wishes. Well, the woman's pretty psyched, and her first wish is for a new sofa. Bam—the fairy gives her not just one sofa, but a whole remodeled living room. Her second wish? A van for transporting her Sunday-school class. Bam— done. Third wish—"

"I apologize in advance for this ending," Stacy said.

"You go right ahead," Grady encouraged.

"Thank you." Dan scowled in his wife's direction. "Anyway, so for the woman's third wish, she thought about it for a good long while, then said, 'Don't suppose all this fancy furniture will do me much good without someone to share it with. Think you could turn my cat into a sexy stud?' Poof! Her cat was suddenly trans- formed into the ultimate hunk—someone not unlike myself."

More groans abounded.

Dan ignored them. "So the woman was thrilled—at least until the cat-hunk said, 'Bet you wish you hadn't had me neutered?' Get it?"

Allen pitched a red Solo cup at their old friend. "That was bad—but funny."

The rest of the evening took on the same lighthearted tone, with plenty of good food, music and laughter.

After the kids had been put to bed, and Angel had fallen asleep nestled against Jessie's chest, Dan was in the midst of telling another epic joke when Jessie felt Grady cup his hand to her bare thigh beneath the table. The gesture might have been small to some, but to her, his simplest touch made her spirit soar while other parts of her hummed with tingly awareness. It didn't make sense, but on this perfect night, logic didn't matter. All that did was the piney scent of piñon smoke from Corny's chimenea and the soft love song playing on the stereo and the first hearty spring crickets' chirps. Of course, all of that would have been quite ordinary without sharing it with Grady and Angel.

Jessie's chest tightened with gratitude for both the man and baby even temporarily being in her life. She couldn't say what compelled her to do it, but all of a sudden she found herself sliding close enough to Grady to rest her head upon his shoulder.

"Aw..." Stacy clasped her hands together and grinned. "Grady and Jessie, you two look just like you did back in high school. When are you finally getting hitched?"

Chapter Thirteen

Jessie bolted upright.

"Um, yeah," Grady said. "As soon as I help Mom and Dad get squared away, I've got to head back to base."

"You seem more like an ordinary cowboy than a Navy SEAL," Kristi said.

"Oh?" Grady finished off his latest beer. "What's a SEAL supposed to look like?"

"I figured you'd walk with a superhero swagger and be all mean and squinty eyed like one of those gun-for-hire movie mercenaries."

Grady chuckled. "See, that's the thing about movie SEALs versus the real deal. Any guy who's truly earned his Trident would never even tell you—although some guys do have a swagger they only pull out on Friday or Saturday nights for the ladies." He winked.

Jessie didn't like thinking of Grady's job. Sure, she was proud of him for serving their country, but the danger element made her nauseous.

"Still," Kristi's husband, Nick, said, "you have to have done some crazy you-know-what. How many terrorists have you plugged?"

"Jeez, Nick." Kristi elbowed him.

"Sorry. I'm curious."

Grady cast the man an unreadable smile, then looked to Angel. "On that note, it's way past this little darlin's bedtime. Jess, you ready to get Angel to her crib?"

"Hey, man," Nick said, "I didn't mean to offend you. There's no need to break up the party."

"No offense taken," Grady assured. To all assembled, he said, "Thanks, guys. This has been great. Let's do it again before I head back to Virginia."

"You bet," Allen said before he and Corny walked them to the door.

After goodbye hugs and getting Angel's diaper bag stowed and settling her in the car seat mounted in Grady's car, Jessie took his keys, telling their hosts that they'd pick up her car in the morning.

"That was fun," Grady said once Jessie turned out of the neighborhood. "But Kristi and Nick pissed me off."

"Really? I never would've known." She shot him a sideways smile.

"Only an idiot would think it a source of personal pride for me that I've killed people. I do what I have to do, but a life's a life. At one point or another, everyone was born and loved, you know?"

She glanced his way again to find his eyes shining. "You okay?"

"I'm good." She sucked in a breath when he put his hand back on her thigh. "But being here, with you, has jolted me away from that world. I feel myself losing my edge—not a good thing in my line of work. I'm always on—like hyperaware. Being in a war zone is like having a twister roaring at you 24/7. After a while, though, the intensity becomes part of you. This time back home, decompressing—I can't tell you how good it's been."

Jessie couldn't help but wonder where this speech was headed. Maybe she didn't want to know.

"In the same regard, the intensity becomes a rush. Real life feels bland. Vanilla." He leaned his head back and sighed. "Might just be the beer talking, but the only time I've felt anywhere near that same kind of adrenaline rush I feel in battle was getting naked with you."

He slid his hand higher and higher, until his fingertips singed the ultrasensitive strip between her panties and inner thigh. She hadn't planned on wearing the same loose cotton shorts and T-shirt she'd worked in all day, and now she especially wished she'd changed into jeans.

"Grady…" Her breath hitched, and she nearly drove off the road when his roving fingers moved even farther beyond her comfort zone and into dangerously superheated territory.

"Pull over."

Oh. My. God. He'd found her sweet spot and lightly rubbed. It took Jessie every shred of her self-control to keep her foot even on the gas. "Wh-what about the baby?"

"Shit." Leaving her high on a crest with no relief in sight, he slowly moved his hand to a more respectable level.

Although Jessie was glad to have Angel in her life, at that moment her still-ravenous body echoed Grady's sentiment.

GRADY HAD GROWN so hard it hurt.

Lucky for him, by the time they reached home his folks had retired to the pool house and Jessie's parents to their room. Angel was still zonked.

Jessie tucked her in, then grabbed her baby monitor before closing her door.

After making out all the way down the hall and into his bed, they tore at each other's clothes.

He wanted to take things slow with her, but he physically couldn't. Her body made him crazy in all the right ways.

"Lord, you're hot," he said once he had her naked and bathed in moonlight and positioned for him to nip and kiss and stroke into the same frenzy she'd caused in him.

"So are you…" She splayed her fingers over his chest, in the process driving him even wilder.

He managed to slow their pace with a more leisurely exploration of her lips.

Lower, he helped himself to the nest between her legs, intent on finishing the job he'd started earlier. She was hot and wet and wild, and when she spread her legs, bucking against him, he eased one finger in, then two, all the while rubbing her hardened nub with his thumb.

He stroked her tongue with his, burying his free hand in her hair. When her breathing turned to frenetic huffs, he felt the rise in her pleasure deep in his own soul. He wanted to give her everything—not just the night of her life, but the ultimate ride she'd carry with her forever.

She stiffened, then moaned. "Please…"

"Just a sec, baby. Let me find a condom."

"Doesn't matter," she said with a shake of her head. Her hair had spilled free of the ponytail she'd worn during dinner and now rested in a lush curtain on his pillow. *"Please…"*

Entering her was like coming home.

The rhythm he established was all at once exhilarating, comforting and familiar. Despite all those years they'd been apart, here they were again. If he had his way, this was how they'd always be.

JESSIE WOKE SLOWLY, at first confused as to where she even was. It dawned on her when she realized Grady's warm, muscular chest currently served as her pillow.

Despite knowing this was probably not her wisest decision, she smiled.

What a night.

If she didn't have kids arriving in her makeshift classroom first thing tomorrow morning, she'd have initiated another round. Unfortunately, thanks to the tornado, she had an absurd amount of prep work to do in a ridiculously inadequate time.

She eased from the bed, trying not to wake Grady. She'd almost made her escape to a hot shower and coffee and the emotional space needed to process what her night spent with Grady meant when he shot his arm out to snag her around her waist.

"Where do you think you're going?" His voice was sleep-husky and warmed her all over again.

"I've got work. And I should check on Angel."

"Is she awake?"

"No, but—"

He sat up in the bed, combing his fingers into her hair, drawing her into the sweetest of kisses. "Good morning."

"Yes, it is," she teased. "But no matter how much I want to stay with you, I have to get in the shower."

"I understand. Need help washing your hair?"

"You offering?"

"Hell, yeah."

She kissed him. "Yes, please."

Not that she was complaining, but by the time they

finished doing a bit more than washing each other's hair, their teeth chattered from having run out of hot water.

Grady turned on the overhead heat lamp, then towel dried her while she stood with her eyes closed, soaking up the pampering. She couldn't remember the last time she'd felt more satiated—if ever—and had him to thank for it.

She landed a kiss to his lips. "Meet you in a sec in Angel's room?"

"Absolutely."

Anticipating another full day of sorting and hauling and bulletin board assembly, she tugged on shorts and a T-shirt. Socks, sneakers and a quick ponytail finished her morning preparation. She missed adding her necklace with Grady's engagement ring, but didn't want him to think that she'd harbored a secret sentimental streak where he was concerned after all this time.

She fed Toby his morning cricket, then washed her hands before making a beeline for Angel's room.

Grady had beaten her to the infant's crib.

Jessie eased alongside him, for once having no problem with their shoulders and hips touching.

"She's beautiful, isn't she?"

"Amazing in every possible way." Jessie drank in the baby's perfection. The way she suckled her tiny fist in her sleep. The way her curls were flat in some spots and springy in others.

When Grady slipped his arm around her waist, Jessie rested her head against his shoulder like she had at Allen and Corny's, only now, without an audience, she felt free to enjoy his company without their friends' questions or expectations.

"Allen said something yesterday—before you showed up. It's got me wondering…"

"About what?"

"He said if no one claims Angel, she'll go into the system. He suggested I go ahead and file for adoption—just in case."

"That's heavy. Are you sure you're ready for instant motherhood?"

"The funny thing is—" she tucked the infant's fuzzy pink blanket back over her bare toes where she'd kicked it off "—ever since the night we picked her up, I can't remember a time when Angel wasn't in my life." *You, too, for that matter.* Sure, she and Grady had had their petty quarrels, and there'd been times his smart mouth had made her feel capable of cheerfully strangling him, but deep down, she was starting to feel fate had, for whatever reason, drawn all three of them together.

"Then, go for it. If you want, when you're done with school this afternoon, I'll get Allen to set up a meeting with someone from the Department of Human Services. We can talk to them together to find out your first step."

"Thanks. I'd like that."

"No problem," he said with a comforting squeeze.

This time when they kissed, there was no urgency, just a particular brand of comfort stemming from a former lifetime's certainty.

For as long as she could remember, they'd been friends. And then, gradually more. When he'd proposed on a senior class trip to Tulsa's Gilcrease Museum, right in front of Bierstadt's *Sierra Nevada Morning*—she remembered, not just because there'd been a question about it on their art final, but because he'd promised to give her a life as beautiful as the painting—it had never even occurred to her to deny his request. Why would she? Even at that tender age, she'd known he was all she'd ever wanted in a man. He'd meet her needs and listen to her and kiss her until she couldn't be sure where she left off and he began.

What's going to happen with us? she wanted to ask when they paused for air. *Are you going to ask me to marry you all over again? Or are you headed back to the Navy? To that intensity you described?* If he did stay, how long would it be until being with her was no longer a rush, but dreaded vanilla?

"YOU'RE AWFULLY QUIET." Grady's dad was back to sorting through rubble on the family ranch for anything of value.

His mother did the same in the area that used to be the master bedroom.

"Don't take it personally," Grady said. Considering the heated night he and Jessie had shared, he hadn't trusted himself to help her out in her classroom, which was why he'd dropped her off, agreeing to pick her up later for their trip to the police station. Besides, the whole reason he'd returned to Rock Bluff hadn't been to get tangled back up with Jessie, but to help his folks rebuild. "Guess I've got a lot on my mind."

"Don't suppose all your thinking involves a perky little blonde?"

Grady snorted. "That woman has a way of boring into my head like a woodpecker through a rotten tree."

"Sorry, son, but that doesn't say much for the health of your head."

"Tell me about it."

They shared a laugh.

Then his dad sobered while stacking an armful of

his mom's miraculously unbroken wedding china on the rain-damaged dining room table they planned to re-finish. "Last time we were out here, you were worried about a little kiss. Why do I get the feeling things may have progressed a bit further?"

Maybe because they have? "Dad, she's got my head spinning. Part of me thinks if she'd have me, I'd retire from the Navy and move back here permanently—help you with the ranch. Get hitched…"

"Sounds good so far—assuming you've had your fill of adventure—but I can tell by that same sulky look you used to get whenever your mom made you get a haircut that something about your plan isn't as idyllic as you'd like."

Am I that transparent? "Remember when I told you she broke things off with me after I proposed, just before we graduated high school?" He plucked a couple brass elephants from the debris.

"Sure. And I told you to take her out for a night under the stars. Am I safe to assume you made progress on your campout?"

"Yes and no. I finally got her to tell me why she wouldn't marry me—only, it wasn't what I expected to hear. She says she can't have kids."

"What?" His dad stopped to wrinkle his nose and rub his lower back. "What's that mean?"

"She's got some condition that makes it so she can't have babies. Guess she had a surgery and tried a couple fancy fertility methods on her own, but nothing worked."

"She can't ever have kids? Meaning, if the two of you got hitched, no grandchildren?"

"Not unless we'd adopt."

His dad grunted. "I'm going to have to sit on this a

spell, then run it past your mom. Jessie's a good girl—the *best*. But, son…" Tears shone in his eyes. "The thought of you never having your own blood kin—well, I s'pose I'd get used to it, but it'd take a while. I'm assuming this is the issue weighing on you?"

"Nah. Honestly, my heart aches for her. You've seen her around Angel—Jessie would make a great mom. I'm already so attached to that little monkey, I might even be past worrying about the whole biological-kid issue."

"Then what's the problem?"

"Honestly?" Grady brushed chalky drywall remains from the thighs of his jeans. "Deep down, I'm scared shitless of quitting the Navy, making another commitment to Jess, then having her bolt all over again. Losing her damn near killed me the first time. If she pulled that stunt a second time?" He bowed his head.

"I get it." His dad cupped his hand to Grady's shoulder. "Pray on it. Think. Then think some more. For the time being, there's no rush. But if the day comes when you decide you do want to give things another go, stop thinking and let your heart decide."

As much as Grady appreciated his dad's advice, all of that was easier said than done. As smitten as he was, he was also that scared.

"Knock, knock."

Jessie glanced up from the welcome-back folders she'd been stuffing to have her heart skip a beat. There was Grady, in all his dark-haired, blue-eyed glory. His good looks had always taken her breath away, but now there seemed to be an extra depth she'd never seen coming.

Maybe because he also held her beautiful Angel?

"Hey, handsome—and gorgeous." She blasted both of them with a smile. What a difference a day made. Yesterday, she'd struggled to keep her hands off Grady. Today, she rose from her chair for a hug. "I'm so excited. I've been waiting all afternoon for this. Hi, pumpkin."

Had she imagined it, or did Angel seem happy to see her?

"Did she smile?" Grady asked.

Jessie laughed. "I was just going to ask you the same question." She jiggled the baby's tiny sneakers. "Are you happy to see me?"

"Aaaaeee," the baby gurgled through an adorable grin.

"Did she just say *Jessie*?" Of course she hadn't, but maybe one day.

"That's what I heard." He winked. "Ready to get this ball rolling?"

"I think so." She forced a deep breath, releasing it slowly. "Thanks again for doing this with me. Since Mom deals with the DHS all the time, I probably should be bringing her, but I want to do this on my own. Does that even make sense?"

"Sure—only you're not on your own, because I'll be with you." When he cupped her cheek, she closed her eyes and leaned into his touch. "Are you sure that's okay?"

"Of course." Because in a perfect world, she and Grady would raise Angel together.

Even though the tent city comprised of cleanup volunteers and National Guard still bustled, the police station lobby was surprisingly quiet.

Allen worked the counter. "Great. You two are here

early and so is Carla—she's our DHS liaison. She's good people. You'll like her."

Jessie smiled, because nerves had closed her throat to the point that she feared she might not be able to speak. She wiped her sweating palms on her calico shorts. Why hadn't she thought to change into a dress—at the very least, slacks and a blouse?

"Thanks, man." On the way to the break room that was by now starting to feel familiar, Grady shook Allen's hand. "I appreciate your help."

"No problem. We all want what's best for this little lady. Barring finding her true parents, I can't think of anyone better suited to care for her than your Jess."

Your Jess.

Jessie noticed Grady didn't correct his old friend. Did that mean he did still view her as his girl? She hoped so. On this day especially, she really hoped so.

Just before entering what could turn out to be her own personal lion's den, he took her hand, drawing her back. His reassuring touch calmed her in a way she knew nothing else could. "Breathe, Jess. This is an exploratory meeting—nothing more."

She nodded, hoping his words of encouragement were true.

"Hi." In the break room, a pretty brunette rose from her seat at the table. She wore purple horn-rimmed glasses and the more professional blouse-and-slacks combo Jessie wished she'd worn. "I'm Carla."

"Sorry about—" Jessie gestured to her outfit. "I'm usually more put together, but I've been working in my new classroom all day—I'm a second-grade teacher and… I'm sorry. I'm rambling."

"Please, sit down. And no worries about your outfit. Your mom has such a stellar record in helping us with emergency cases that meeting with you today is a formality. Here are the legalities." She shoved a pile of paperwork across the table toward Jessie. "Officially, the infant will be in the state foster care system for the next fifteen months. If, at the end of that period, her parents—or other blood relations willing to assume custody—still haven't been located, then you will be first in line to file for formal adoption. In the meantime, since technically your mother is on the books as the infant's primary caregiver, you'll need to attend twenty-seven hours of bridge-parenting classes and undergo a standard background check that will allow us to place you in the foster-parent system. As long as you have your own car, a suitable home and are a nonsmoker, then I can get the ball rolling today."

"Great. Thank you." Jessie wanted to be ecstatic, but fifteen months was a long time for the fear of losing the baby to crush her chest.

"Oh—thank *you*. We're always on the hunt for conscientious foster parents—but just to be clear, please understand that with any case, our agency's primary goal is to reunite children with their birth parents, especially in a heartbreaking case like this. Obviously, with an infant this adorable, you'll find it all too easy to fall in love, but should her parents return, you'll need to turn over custody immediately. Are we clear?"

Jessie somehow managed to swallow, then nodded.

Chapter Fourteen

"That was depressing." Grady held the office building's door open for Jessie to pass through. It had been a week since their meeting with the DHS rep, and he'd sat with Jessie through her first Saturday-afternoon foster-parenting class and found it to be not at all what he'd expected.

"Agreed."

It was raining, and they dashed down the sidewalk to his car, only a UPS truck had parked behind it with its hazard lights blinking.

"Starbucks?" he shouted above what had turned into a downpour. He pointed to the adjoining shopping center, then took her hand, tugging her toward shelter.

After taking a stab at drying themselves with napkins, they gave up and ordered coffees and two slices of carrot cake before grabbing a corner table.

"There he goes." Grady pointed out the window at the UPS driver pulling away.

"We might as well stay here till the rain lets up. After all those sobering statistics, I could use a cake break." Jessie winked before digging into her sweet treat and coffee. "I see why Mom only takes in the smaller kiddos, but my heart breaks for the older ones. Some of those case studies…" She pressed her hand to her chest. "They were so sad."

"In happier news, my mom said Billy Sue told her Rock Bluff is hosting a Memorial Day picnic. Apparently, the city council wants to celebrate all the volunteers who've helped out, and remind people that the town might be gone, but hamburgers and hot dogs live on."

"Nice." She sipped her coffee, then made a face.

"What's wrong?"

"I don't know." Her gaze moved to her cup. "This isn't setting well. I think I'm going to—" Before she could even finish her sentence, she dashed for the bathroom. When she tried the handle on the ladies' room and found it locked, she darted into the men's.

Grady took her purse from where she'd left it on the extra chair at their table to stand outside the restroom door. "Jess? You okay?"

The moans from inside didn't sound good.

"Babe? Is there anything I can do?" He waited for what seemed like a month before hearing the sink run.

She finally emerged.

"What the hell? Are you okay?"

She nodded. "I don't know what happened. I mean, obviously I won't be eating carrot cake any time soon, but sheesh."

"How are you feeling now?"

"All right. Sort of. I really just want to take a nap. That class took a lot out of me. Hearing the grim realities of the foster-care system makes me feel guilty for not helping more."

"Yeah, well…" He paused by their table to toss their leftovers and cups in the trash. "For now, let's just get you home to check on Angel."

Halfway to the car, she asked, "What if I've caught a bug? I don't want to get her sick."

"Then, me or your mom or my mom will check on her. You just take it easy. If it is a virus, hopefully it passes soon."

THANKFULLY, BY MONDAY, Jessie did feel better, but the mere smell of coffee in the supply-closet-turned-teacher's-lounge made her stomach churn.

Back in her classroom, she steeled herself for her students' return from afternoon recess. Usually, she adored her job, but in the too-small space it was tough to maneuver and the children, many of whom had lost their homes, struggled to maintain focus. Three of her students hadn't even come back, as their families had chosen to relocate rather than rebuild.

"Miss Long! Look what I found under a bush!" One of her favorites, plump little Henry Rice, held up a DVD case. The cover was not the sort of thing appropriate for a second-grader—or even most adults! "I can read it, too. It says *Big*—"

Jessie snatched the case from his chubby hands. "Thank you, sweetie, for bringing this to me. I'll put it in a safe place."

"Can we watch it?"

His classmates entered the room, transforming the quiet space into a frenzy of giggling and talking and scraping of chairs.

"Not today," she said. "Go ahead and sit down. We're going to talk about our soft and hard vowel sounds, and how they work with the letter *C*." In light of the DVD's adult nature, and the way she and Grady had spent their night, her cheeks flamed.

Once everyone had settled, save for the fidgeting that rarely came to a full stop, Jessie said, "Helpers, would you please give a copy of this worksheet to everyone."

Once that task was accomplished, she took her copy marked with her lesson notes to the front of the room. "I know we've been over this at the start of the year, but a lot of you are still having trouble, so I want to be sure everyone understands. Who can tell me what a soft vowel sound is?"

Six hands shot up.

"Hannah, what do you think it is?"

"A soft vowel is like one of those *giant* pretzels you get at the Oklahoma Thunder games."

"Not exactly, but thanks for making me hungry. Anyone else want to tell me?" Jessie inwardly groaned. This was one of those times that, as a teacher, she wasn't sure whether to laugh or cry. "Terry—what do you think it is?"

He wrinkled his nose. "I think it's when the sounds of the vowels change when they have different continents."

"Perfect—except, I think you mean *consonants*?"

"Yeah, I meant that." He grinned, reminding her why she loved her job.

"Awesome. So who wants to give us an example of a hard and then a soft vowel sound?"

This time, ten wriggling boys' and girls' arms shot up.

"Desiree, what are your examples?"

"Well…" She touched her tongue almost to her nose.

A knock sounded on Jessie's open classroom door.

She glanced that way to find Grady with Angel in his arms. A warm flush took hold of her senses, flooding her with well-being. Had there ever been two more gorgeous beings?

"Aw, look at the baby!" Hannah squirmed from her chair for a closer inspection.

She was soon followed by a fairly civilized stampede of other curious little people.

"Sorry," Grady said. "I didn't mean to interrupt."

"It's okay. Let me wrangle these kiddos back to their seats and get them started on their worksheet, then we can talk in the hall."

Five minutes later, with her students focused on their assignment, she rejoined Grady just outside her room.

"What's up?" she asked, taking Angel from him for a quick cuddle.

He withdrew folded papers from his back pocket. "I was headed to Norman for a few things Dad needs from Lowe's, and your mom asked me to give you these. She says you need to sign them right away."

"What are they for?"

"Don't know."

A quick glance showed them to be copies of the initial foster-parenting forms she'd already completed. She sighed. "What they are is I'm guessing another one of my mother's matchmaking attempts. I've already turned these in—if I hadn't, I wouldn't have been able to start my class hours."

"Sorry," Grady said. "So I basically interrupted you for nothing?"

"Pretty much, but—" she kissed Angel's cheek "—I'm not complaining." On her tiptoes, reasonably sure no one was watching, she stole a kiss from Grady, too.

"Mmm! Miss Long is kissing!"

Heat surged to her cheeks.

Grady stepped back and cleared his throat. "This is awkward."

"Is he your boyfriend?" Terry shouted.

"Kid asks a legit question," Grady said. "Am I? Your boyfriend?"

Jessie couldn't think. Her head told her to say no, but her still-tingling lips said, "Yes. You're my boyfriend. Now get out of here, before my principal catches us and I get fired."

He took Angel. "You know this means you and this cutie are now my official dates for the Memorial Day picnic, right?"

"We'd better be," she teased, wanting to kiss him again, but regrettably refraining. "Or else…"

"I'm liking this whole mean-teacher vibe you're working. We'll have to explore this side of you tonight, because I might be a *very* bad boy." He winked, and then worked Angel's arm to help the baby wave goodbye.

Jessie finally got her students settled down and once again focused on their work, but she couldn't keep her own mind from Grady's naughty suggestion.

CONSIDERING JESSIE'S CURRENT overheated status, Memorial Day might as well have been the Fourth of July. She snatched an extra paper plate from the buffet line to use as a fan.

"Warm?" Grady asked. He held Angel in a backpack-style carrier.

She fanned faster. "You're not?"

He shook his head. "Let's just say there's no heat quite like the Middle East. Plain old Oklahoma sun doesn't faze me."

"All right, so I'm a wimp." They moved forward in the endless snaking line.

"You're perfect." He kissed her—right there in front of God and everyone. While she probably should have pushed him away, she'd have rather pulled him closer, daydreaming about how everything in her life would change for the better should Grady decide to stay. He would make an amazing father for Angel—or any child. But then, if Jessie hadn't already known that on a soul-deep level, she never would have broken up with him in the first place. The last thing she'd wanted was to deprive him of what she'd always dreamed of, and with Angel, was finally experiencing firsthand—the magic of parenthood.

"You're pretty amazing yourself." She returned his kiss. The ardent pressure of his lips against hers did little to help regulate her temperature, but she wasn't complaining. Suddenly, her life felt so perfect it scared her. "Do you think Angel's birth parents will be found?"

"No. I'm not sure what happened, but if they were out there, I think they'd have stepped forward before now."

She nodded. The notion that she received such joy from someone else's unimaginable tragedy was disconcerting. She didn't like thinking of herself in that light. "During our foster-parenting class, when the instructor talked about abandoned infants, I wondered if that could have been what happened to Angel's mom. What if she's out there somewhere, but for whatever reason didn't think she could raise her child?"

The line inched forward, and they took silverware and napkins.

"That's as good an explanation as any."

"I think so, too." Which, in a small way, made her

feel better—as if she weren't taking Angel from someone, but instead taking the responsibility they'd viewed as a burden to transform the situation into a blessing.

They'd finally reached the side dishes—coleslaw and macaroni, potato and bean salads. Deviled eggs and baked beans and soft cloverleaf rolls.

Ravenous, Jessie filled her plate with a little of everything. At the main courses, she heaped even more onto her plate. Smoked brisket and bologna and a hot dog on a bun with only mustard.

By the time they'd reached the desserts, her plate was too full for anything else—at least for now.

"It's about time the three of you showed up," Billy Sue said when Jessie, Grady and Angel wound their way through the crowd to the gingham-covered picnic table deep in the shade of Colonel Jefferson Monroe's memorial park. He'd fought in the civil war on the side of the Confederates, but his wife had been a Yankee. She'd donated the land and statue to the city upon his death.

One of the park's newest additions—a whitewashed gazebo-style bandstand—had survived the storm, and a banjo trio now played patriotic songs.

While Jessie's dad fed Cotton nibbles of his hamburger, supposedly to energize him for the upcoming dog beauty contest, her mother flipped through note cards while practicing her upcoming speech.

In the shade, Jessie's internal thermometer thankfully cooled, but when she looked at her heaped plate, she was struck with nausea. She pushed it away.

"What're you doing?" Grady asked. "Thought you were starving?" He'd hefted Angel from her carrier, and now cradled her to his chest.

The infant whimpered.

"I can't eat if Angel's hungry." Call her crazy, but the longer Jessie was around Angel, the more she seemed able to decode her varied cries.

"I can feed her if you want to dig in," he offered.

"Thanks, but let me take her." She unearthed a pre-made bottle from Angel's baby bag then took her from Grady. The exchange warmed her all over again, but for different reasons. Merely brushing her arms against his reminded her of their private times together and how much she was enjoying getting to know him all over again in the most intimate way a man and woman could.

Angel contentedly latched on to the bottle.

What would it feel like to breastfeed? The bonding experience had to be incredible. But then, so was this. The way Angel stared so intently into Jessie's eyes, as if forming a mental imprint of her features. All around them the park teemed with life—children laughing, banjos playing, her mother being told by Floyd from the city council that it was almost time for her speech. Yet Jessie, despite all of this, felt that she and Angel and Grady might as well have been on their own private island. Could it be her sudden bouts of nausea had nothing to do with her stomach, but rather with her mind? Was it a reflection of the apprehension that consumed her when she thought about just how much she'd grown to need Angel and Grady in her life, and how fragile those bonds really were?

At any given time, Angel's parents could step forward, or Grady could choose to leave. It wasn't emotionally wise for her to place her future happiness on the head of a pin, but did she have any other choice?

She was already halfway across the tightrope spanning a canyon. At this point, she could turn back, or force a deep breath and carefully inch her way across. Essentially, the choice was hers—only, it wasn't. She couldn't control Angel's family or Grady staying or going. Which was why even the scent of the hamburgers being cooked by volunteer fireman on their grill had her fighting a fresh round of nausea.

"Jessie, honey, are you okay?" From across the table, Rose gazed upon her with concern. "You're white as a sheet."

"I'm good," Jessie said, wishing it were true.

Through the crowd, she saw her mother's strong, reassuring form marching onto the bandstand, where she took a handheld mic. Feedback caused her to jump, and then laugh.

The crowd shared her smile.

"Dang," Billy Sue said with her hand pressed to her chest. "That about scared the ants right off my potato salad."

After a few more jokes to loosen up the friends and neighbors she'd been around most of her life, as well as the hundreds of volunteers and National Guard members still in town, she thanked everyone who'd helped with the picnic, then got down to business. "While the meaning of Memorial Day is to remember, what I'd like for us to do as a community is to not so much forget, but put this whole nasty tornado business behind us. Yes, we can acknowledge the pain and the fact that not a single one of us escaped that monster without loss. Maybe your car, or business or home—God forbid some of you out there lost all three and a loved one. This recovery is a nasty, heartbreaking job that, unfortunately, we still have a long way to go in completing. But what all of you gathered here today prove is that the fine folks of Rock Bluff might be down, but no one better dare count us out!"

The audience cheered—save for one old hound that bayed instead.

"All right, so now that the sappy stuff's out of the way, in about twenty minutes or so we're gonna get down and dirty with some competitions. Maumel's Trophy Shop has donated prizes, and trust me, you're not gonna want to leave without one!"

"Billy Sue did such a nice job," Rose said before biting into a brownie.

"She sure did," Ben noted.

Roger took out his earbuds. "What?"

"Dad!" Jessie scolded. "Didn't you hear Mom's speech?"

"Sorry, but the Cardinals are playing. Lord knows I've heard your momma pontificate on many occasions."

Grady didn't bother trying to hide his chuckle, so she elbowed his ribs.

The afternoon bobbed along. Wheelbarrow races led to the judging of the dog beauty contest—Cotton, decked out in formalwear, bit a Yorkie and was disqualified.

Billy Sue marched toward their shady glade.

Judging by her scowl, she was not happy with Cotton's politically incorrect behavior. "Why are you such a bad boy?" she said to her fuzzy white pet while holding him out to Jessie. "Could you please watch him? I have to judge the pie-eating contest. Oh—and don't let your father feed him any more table scraps. He threw up on the doggy runway red carpet."

With her mother charging off to her next event and her dad snoring in sun-dappled shade with Angel in her carrier alongside him, Jessie dug through the picnic hamper for Cotton's leash. No way was she going to hold the yappy little furball for the rest of the afternoon.

Grady was once again laughing. "Your family cracks me up."

"I'm glad we can amuse you, but for the record, have you looked at yours?" She nodded toward the pie-eating table, where his dad was devouring a cherry pie with no hands while normally mild-mannered Rose wildly cheered him on.

He groaned. "Is that going to be us in thirty years?"

Her heart skipped a beat. "I—I suppose it could be. If, I mean, well...you'd want it to be."

He rose from his seat at the picnic table, settling his big hands low on her hips. For what felt like forever, he stared into her eyes while her foolish heart hammered.

"Hypothetically speaking..."

He just kept staring. *What are you thinking behind your gorgeous sky-blue eyes, Grady Matthews?*

"Not that I was suggesting we actually..." While her words trailed into the ether, she wasn't sure what to do with her hands. She settled the dilemma by pressing them to Grady's solid chest.

Why wasn't he talking? Why, beneath her palms, did his heart race as quickly as her own?

"Marry me," he said in a voice so low she couldn't be sure his words weren't just the wind.

"What?" Her pulse took off on a wild canter.

"You heard me. Jessie Anne Long..." He slipped his warm, strong fingers beneath her sundress's collar, tugging the chain she'd put on especially for today. "I wondered if you'd been lying about losing my ring, and then the other day when we were feeding Toby, I saw this in your jewelry box. Looks as if you were telling a tall tale?"

Too dazed to speak, she nodded.

He slipped the chain over her head, then unlatched it, allowing the engagement ring he'd given her all those years ago to slip off. He tried putting it on her ring finger, but to her mortification, it barely fit up to her knuckle.

Laughing, he said, "Oops, looks as if someone's lost her girlish figure." Leaning closer, he kissed her neck. His hot string of kisses made her shiver despite the heat. Switching the ring to her left pinkie finger, he said, "Good thing I prefer a woman with curves."

"Grady..." Her cheeks blazed while she checked to ensure her father was still asleep.

"Well? We'll go pick you out a new ring, but until then, can I at least have an answer?"

"What about the Navy?"

"I'll file for an early discharge. I miss ranching. You, me and Angel will live the life we've always dreamed of. Hell, we'll take in foster kids and pack our place full of children. It doesn't matter where they come from. We'll love them all the same."

Tears burned her eyes. She tried holding them back, but the effort proved too much.

"Jess, I'm dying here. Yes or no?"

Chapter Fifteen

Grady was happier than a prairie dog in soft dirt.

Not only had Jessie said yes to his proposal, but they'd decided seven years had been a long enough engagement, and were planning a late-June wedding before he was due back on base to complete his current enlistment agreement. Since she was currently homeless, she'd accompany him. They'd find a little two-bedroom for the three of them, and once he was discharged, they'd return to Rock Bluff. He had some money saved up, and had already talked to his parents' builder about putting in the house he'd always wanted, with a front-yard view of the catfish pond.

It was Jessie's last day of school. He was currently on his way to pick her up. That morning, when he'd dropped her off, her mood had been bittersweet. She'd had to tell her principal she wouldn't be returning for the new school year. As much as she loved her job, she'd understandably struggled with the decision. Fortunately for him and Angel, she loved them more.

At a stoplight, he glanced in the rearview mirror at the gurgling infant. She happily gnawed a teething ring he'd had to snatch from Cotton, then sanitize.

He completed the short drive to the church, parked,

then swooped Angel from her car seat onto his shoulders. "Ready to find your mom?"

She cooed before gumming his hair.

"Hey..." he complained, tickling her chubby tummy. "No munching on your father."

He perched on a wooden bench, enjoying the warm sun when the Sunday school's double doors burst open and wild-eyed kids freed for the summer stampeded through.

Smiling, he said to his soon-to-be-official daughter, "That's going to be you one of these days—only by the time you start kindergarten, a brand-new school will have been built."

Once the initial flurry of activity died down, he and Angel strolled to Jessie's room, only to find her standing at her desk in tears.

"Hey..." He went to her for an awkward one-armed hug, since he needed his other arm to hold the baby. "What's wrong?"

"S-saying goodbye to my students was so hard. It is every year, but this year, knowing I won't be back—"

"We'll only be in Virginia a year, and your principal already told you that you're first in line for an opening when you get back."

"I know." She sniffed. "But it's still hard."

"Babe..." He tipped her chin up so she'd meet his gaze. "If you want to stay here while I finish, I'd understand. I mean, I'd miss you and Angel like hell, but we'll get through it."

She shook her head. "I fought too hard for this little family to lose even part of it now. I'll be fine. Besides, Angel's already lost one set of parents. It's important for her to bond with both of us."

"Agreed." Lord, he loved this woman. He kissed her hard enough for her to know that even after all these years, he was still crazy about her, but softly enough for her to realize she now held the title of most precious person in his life, with Angel coming in right on her heels.

A man at the door cleared his throat.

Grady stopped kissing his soon-to-be wife to find her grinning boss.

"Sorry to interrupt, Jessie, but I wanted to reassure you that just as soon as you're back, you'll have a job at Rock Bluff Elementary—might be in the school kitchen until a teaching position opens up, but we'll find something for you."

"Aw, thanks." Laughing through a fresh batch of tears, she gave the portly man a hug. "I think?"

"No more tears." The principal took a tissue from a box on a nearby bookshelf and handed it to her. "You're going to have the time of your life. Everyone needs to leave their hometown long enough to realize how much they love it. You'll be back before you know it. And by then, you'll not only have a new school, but new house for this cutie." He wiggled Angel's sandal-covered foot.

After blowing her nose, Jessie asked, "You are coming to our wedding, right?"

"Wouldn't miss it for the world."

Grady's smile was so big it hurt. When it came to the topic of finally marrying the only woman he'd ever loved, he felt exactly the same—he wouldn't miss spending the rest of his life with her and their miracle baby for the world.

"IF YOU WANT CHOCOLATE," Jessie said Friday at the Norman confection shop that was baking their wedding cake, "then I don't see why you can't have a separate groom's cake. That's what Allen and Corny had at their reception." The wedding was June 27—a mere three weeks from Saturday. "I swear, if you keep fighting me on every detail, we're not even going to have a wedding."

"Oh—there *will* be a wedding," he said. "And there will also be a chocolate layer. I don't see why it's a problem for us to just add one more layer. That way, you get your lemon chiffon, strawberry champagne and traditional white."

"You two, simmer down." Rose held Angel, and she covered her little ears to deliver a scolding. "There's no sense in making a fuss."

"I couldn't agree more," Billy Sue said.

"Okay, fine," Jessie said, more out of her need for fresh air than because she agreed with the decision. Her nausea was worse than ever. "Have your stupid chocolate layer, but if half the town laughs at us, you're shouldering all the blame."

Her groom rolled his eyes.

"Jessie Anne Long," her mother said, "what's the matter with you? Lately, you've been about as contrary as a wet cat. This is going to be your one and only wedding. Would it hurt you to occasionally smile?"

Jessie bared her teeth. "I'm sorry. I'm tired and can't seem to shake this bug. I'm either starving or nauseous—never a nice, pleasant in-between."

Rose patted Jessie's hand. "I was a nervous bride. I almost left Ben at the altar, but I'd never been on vacation and *really* wanted that Niagara Falls honeymoon."

"It's not that I'm nervous," Jessie said while the cake decorator went to get her book of sample cakes. "I just don't feel good."

"Think you should go to the doctor?" Billy Sue asked.

"I will if I'm still not better before we leave for Virginia. I just don't have time right now. This wedding might be rushed, but I want every detail to be perfect."

"It will be," her mother assured.

Jessie shot Grady a look. "Not if my groom has any more to do with it. Did you know he wanted our colors to be orange and black?"

"Grady Lynn Matthews." Now Rose was casting him her own dirty look. "Please tell me Jessie's kidding."

"What's wrong with orange and black?" He popped another chocolate cake sample into his mouth. "Everyone loves Halloween. Why not celebrate in June? Our guests could be in costume. Hell, Jess could wear some black Elvira get-up with lots of cleavage, and I could be a vampire. Angel could be Baby Frankenstein. It would be epic."

His mother smacked him on the back of his entirely too-handsome head.

THAT NIGHT, AFTER bathing Angel and tucking her into her crib with Grady's assistance, Jessie turned to Groomzilla and rested her head against his chest. "I'm exhausted. Which of the three florists did you like best?"

"Since you outlawed my Halloween theme, I like that lady who suggested the Western theme with the daisies—especially if you're still okay with getting hitched by the catfish pond, then having the reception in a big tent where the new house will be."

"I think so. I mean, the churches we've seen in Oklahoma City and Norman have all been beautiful, but not really us. I want to be married here, in Rock Bluff. Since our family church is gone, we might as well get married in the biggest cathedral of all, right?"

He rewarded her idea with a kiss. "Sounds perfect. Even better, I'd get to marry you in jeans and my favorite boots, right?"

His hopeful grin made her laugh. "You know, that's actually a cute idea. Only, how about if we split the difference? Brand-new Wranglers and fancy boots on the bottom, and a nice dinner jacket and shirt on top."

"No dorky bow tie?"

"Nope—although, for the record, I think they're nice. Oh—and how about a new cowboy hat? You'd look sexy in a black ten-gallon."

"Wait—" He kissed her, but then pulled back. "I thought you said I couldn't wear black?"

"All right, black hat and boots, but that's it. We're not having black balloons and streamers like you'd originally planned, Dracula. Let's tone it down to a partial Johnny Cash."

"I love you." He kissed her so completely she felt his appreciation for her clear to her toes.

"I love you, too. We're going to have an amazing life."

"Yes, we are."

As they stood arm in arm, watching over their miracle baby, Jessie swallowed what was becoming an all-too-familiar knot in her throat. This kind of bone-deep happiness felt as foreign to her as it did fantastical, but she wasn't complaining.

And to think, fourteen months from now, not only would they be married and in a brand-new house, but Angel would officially, legally, be theirs—not that the baby didn't already belong to Jessie in her heart.

"Why can't I go?" Grady complained the next morning when Jessie and their moms were leaving for wedding dress shopping without him. Might sound crazy, but he was thoroughly enjoying all things wedding. "I promise, if you find the right one, I'll only take a little peek."

"That's my point." She spritzed on the sweet floral perfume that made him want to strip off the sundress she'd only just put on. "Have you been living under a rock, and never heard that it's bad luck for the groom to see the wedding dress before the ceremony?"

"That's BS." He snagged her around her waist for a kiss. "Please, can I tag along? I want to be your naughty dressing room attendant."

"Now you for sure can't come."

Grady was disappointed but in the end let her have her way, settling in with the men of the house for an afternoon of Cardinals versus Cubs baseball on TV. Last time he'd run to the Norman Walmart for his mom, he'd picked up a baby baseball uniform that Angel now wore.

"She sure is a cutie," his dad said during the fifth-inning break. "Just between you and me, after that tornado, I was feeling pretty defeated, but now I'm kind of jazzed about the new barn, and having you—and soon Jessie, and even this little gal—home where you belong."

"Thanks, Dad." Ben wasn't an overly sentimental man, so his words meant a lot. The storm may have wiped Rock Bluff off the map, but for Grady, it had only changed his life for the better. "Better not let Mom hear you're only excited about the barn. Being around Billy Sue so much has made her feisty."

"Sorry," Roger said with a snort, helping himself to the chips and salsa his wife had set out on the coffee table. "My beloved has a way of getting everyone all riled up."

"It's okay." Ben scooped guacamole with his latest chip, then winked. "I'm liking Rose's new wild side."

Grady let that sink in for a second, then winced.

Angel had fallen asleep in her carrier, and he couldn't help but think about what life would be like when she'd grown into a beautiful young woman. Would she have similar conversations with Jessie?

He'd just headed to the john when his cell rang.

"Hey, Allen. What's up?"

"I don't even know how to say this, but I'm gonna need you and Jessie to come down to the station. I think we've found Angel's parents."

Grady lowered his phone.

Allen was still talking, but his voice sounded tinny and funneled.

No. Grady didn't believe it. Not after all this time.

He bent at his waist, fisting the phone, bracing his hands on his knees. His temperature flashed hot, then cold.

He had to think.

Just as if he were trapped behind the border of some godforsaken country, surrounded by enemies, he couldn't lose his shit. What if like the last time, this turned out be a false alarm?

On the flip side, if this turned out to be the real deal and Angel's family had actually been found, for her, that was a wonderful thing. If he loved her as much as he claimed, he could never regret this reunion.

Straightening, he squared his shoulders and hardened his jaw.

In the living room, he said, "Dad, Roger, would you mind watching the baby for a little while? I've got to run a quick errand."

"No problem," Roger said. "But would you mind grabbing more beer on your way home?"

"Sure. Any particular brand?"

"With this Mexican spread, how about Corona?"

"You've got it." Grady forced a smile. "Be right back."

"Chips, too," his dad called out.

Grady was close to losing it, but he managed to say, "I'll grab chips, too."

Before leaving, he glanced at the infant he'd already come to think of as his daughter. She still napped in her carrier, looking as adorable as ever.

Since it was inconceivable to Grady that Angel would ever *not* be in his and Jessie's lives, he refused to give way to the panic lurking in the shadowy recesses of his mind. Now was not the time to question how he'd let himself fall so hard, so fast for both the girls in his life.

Behind the wheel, he calmly, rationally drove to the police station.

He'd get this mess cleared up before Jessie and their moms even got home. There was no need to even tell her about it. He didn't want their wedding day clouded by worry if this was another false alarm.

At the station, Allen left the counter to lead Grady not to the relaxed break room where they'd historically met to discuss Angel's situation, but to a more sterile conference area. The only remarkable features beyond a sea of beige walls and flooring were a table with eight straight-backed chairs, and county road maps haphazardly pinned to a bulletin board.

"Have a seat," Allen said. "Can I get you a coffee? Coke?"

"No." While his old friend closed the door behind them, Grady folded his arms.

"Okay…" Allen walked to the head of the table where

Grady noticed a man's wallet in a plastic bag. "Wow, I'm not even sure where to start. The guys thought this would be best coming from me—you know, on account of us being friends."

"If you think this is the real deal—make it quick." Grady wanted to believe he was strong, but never had he felt more out of control. "It's tough believing that after all this time, we're losing our girl."

"That's just it, man." Allen sighed. "Angel's never been yours—not technically. That's why the foster-parent system has the fifteen-month rule in place. These kinds of things happen. This morning, the National Guard started clearing a heavy section of rubble located on the I-35 access road. They came across a vehicle with Kansas plates. A badly decomposed couple was found inside. The car had been catapulted onto the roof of a storage facility, and an Arby's was blown on top of that. We found Angel in the adjoining field. How she survived—well, it really was a miracle. The car's pretty mangled, but we found a baby bag and some toys and loose bottles. The couple's names were Lena and Doug Griffin. Medical records show their infant's name to be Iris Marie—named after her father's deceased mother. Wichita police have tracked down their next of kin, and the infant's maternal grandmother, Idabelle Martin, is on her way to claim the infant, who is her only remaining relative. Of course, all of this is pending a match of the infant's DNA results against the deceased and Iris's grandmother, but Doug Griffin carried a half-dozen snapshots of the baby you've named Angel in his wallet. Lena also had some in an album in her purse. Would you like to see the photos?"

"No." Grady had witnessed teammates being gunned

down in front of him whose loss had somehow hurt less. His instant love for Angel didn't make sense. The baby wasn't his blood, but somehow his affection for her had woven in and around his feelings for Jessie, until the two of them had become so firmly entrenched in his life that he couldn't remember a time when he hadn't loved them both.

"I know this has to be hard for you, but there are tons of other kids out there who need homes."

Since Grady didn't trust himself not to blow, he simply turned from his friend to leave the room, the station. He had to get back to Angel, and to figure out how the hell he would break the news to Jessie without breaking her.

"Grady." Allen followed him out of the station. "Stay close to your phone. Wichita police did us a solid, and are fast-tracking Miss Martin's DNA results so we can determine if it's a rightful custody claim. As soon as that information comes through, we'll need you to surrender the child."

"I get it, okay?" Grady didn't mean to snap at his old friend, but he felt perilously close to losing control.

"Don't do anything stupid."

"Seriously? Like me and Jess running to Canada with the baby so we can live the rest of our lives looking over our shoulders? You know me better than that, so do me a favor and don't insult me by *ever* bringing up something so asinine again."

"Hey…" Allen held up his hands. "Don't shoot the messenger, man. Crazier shit has happened."

Grady just stared down his friend and shook his head. "Yeah, well, not with me. Call when you hear about the

DNA—but only call me. I don't want Jessie to hear about this through the back door."

"Will do." Allen held out his hand for Grady to shake, but Grady couldn't do it. He couldn't play nice when his world was crumbling. His only hope for escaping this with minimal fallout was for Idabelle Martin's custody claim for Angel to be disproved. But what kind of monster would that make him, to wish for the woman's sole remaining family to not actually be hers?

Chapter Sixteen

"I don't know," Jessie checked out her side view in the dress shop's three-way mirror. "I love this one, but that last strapless number was awfully pretty, too. Mom? Rose? Corny? Help."

Billy Sue cocked her head. "I was thinking I liked the princess neckline with the capped sleeves best. Rose? Which was your favorite?"

"Gosh—" Rose leaned forward "—with Jessie's fancy cowboy boots, I loved that old-fashioned one that was all lacy and had the skirt high in front, long in back."

"You guys are supposed to be helping," Jessie complained, "but all you're really doing is making this harder. Corny, you might as well chime— What's wrong?" Her friend had been reading a text, but she dropped her phone to her lap and paled.

"Nothing." She averted her gaze.

"Something had to have happened. You looked fine just a minute ago, and now..."

Genuinely concerned, Jessie tried taking Corny's phone, but her friend snatched it back. "Really, it's probably nothing."

"Then, why are you being so secretive? Is everything all right with Allen and the kids?"

"Of course." Corny smiled and nodded. "Now, hurry and try on your next dress. I'm still waiting to see my favorite."

"But..." Why was Corny acting to strangely? Since they'd been little girls, they'd told each other everything.

"Leave her alone," Billy Sue said. "Bank of Oklahoma opened a temporary trailer and need me at the ribbon cutting by two."

Jessie abided by her mother's wishes, but couldn't shake the feeling that her friend was upset. By what, she had no idea, but it hurt her feelings that Corny—her matron of honor—was all of a sudden so closemouthed.

For Jessie, the incident spoiled what was supposed to have been a happy occasion.

She didn't find a dress, but they all agreed to meet up on Monday afternoon for a trek to an Oklahoma City shop.

Back at her parents' house—Rose had gone with Billy Sue to the ribbon cutting—Jessie wanted to be with Grady and Angel. They grounded her, and would chase away the gloom that Corny's dour mood had induced.

"Where're Grady and the baby?" she asked her father, whom she found in his recliner with Cotton napping on his lap.

"Not sure," her dad said, looking around her to focus on the baseball game he watched on TV.

"Have you checked out by the pool?" Ben suggested.

"No," she said, "but I will. Thanks."

Outside, sun blazed against the concrete pool deck. Jessie held her hand to her forehead, shading her eyes against the glare.

She saw Grady holding Angel in the swing, but something about his posture wasn't right. His normal pose emanated confidence. He typically sat square and erect. But now, he'd hunched over Angel in what Jessie could only describe as a protective hold.

"Hey," she called on her way to him.

"How was the dress shopping?" He still hadn't looked up from the baby.

"Awful. Not only did I not find a dress, but Corny got a text that clearly shook her up, and she wouldn't tell me what happened. The whole thing gave me the creeps. But now that I'm home with my two favorite people, she can have her secrets, and I'll have a great time enjoying..." Jessie's words trailed off when Grady finally met her gaze.

His blue eyes were red-rimmed and tears lined his cheeks.

She fell to her knees in front of him. "What happened? You're scaring me. Was Allen or one of their kids in an accident?"

"Nope." His lips curved into the oddest smile. "But what kind of person would that make me to selfishly wish they had?"

"Grady..." Covering his hands, she asked, "Please, tell me what's going on. First Corny was upset, and now you? You two are seriously freaking me out."

"I'm freaking myself out. There has been some news." While wiping his eyes with the heels of his hands, he cradled the baby atop his closed legs. "I'm sure Corny didn't mean to shut you out. She probably just wanted you to enjoy your day."

"Seriously, what's wrong?" Her stomach clenched in dread.

"I can't bring myself to say the words."

"Grady...did you get called back to the Navy? Are

you going somewhere dangerous, and you just found out today?"

"I wish." He stood, clutching Angel to him as if he was drowning and she was his only hope. "Angel's family…"

Realization rolled in low and ominous—like distant thunder or ground-hugging fog. It billowed and churned inside her, clawing at her throat. No. After all this time, had Angel's parents stepped forward? "If another couple are claiming custody of Angel, I refuse to believe it. It's just another hoax. They have no proof. The DNA will show police they're lying."

"Stop, Jess. This time it's different. Angel's real name is Iris Marie Griffin. Her parents are dead. Allen said a couple of National Guard volunteers found them in thick rubble. They carried pictures of their baby—our baby."

"But if they're dead…" Hot, messy tears fell, yet her pain sprang from a well so deep Jessie hadn't realized she'd been crying. "She'll need us to watch over her."

"Her grandmother is on the way. She should be here sometime late tonight or tomorrow."

"No. I'm not giving Angel to anyone. She's mine— *ours.*" Of course, Jessie knew her words were irrational, but so was her love for this tiny creature. She took the baby from Grady to nestle her against her chest. In her arms, Angel was warm and sleepy and smelled impossibly sweet.

Jessie's throat ached as if she'd swallowed gravel.

She glanced up to find Grady's expression unreadable. He'd slipped on a cold, aloof mask she found impenetrable.

"I've got to go," he said.

"Where?" *I need you.*

"Just away. I need to run. Think."

"Please..." She didn't know what she wanted from him—maybe just more. More hugging and empathy and caring. Where was the man she knew? The man she would soon marry? She didn't recognize this hard shell.

He didn't even look back at her when he said, "I've got my cell. I'll be back when Allen calls, telling us it's time to hand over the baby."

GRADY CHARGED UPSTAIRS to grab his keys.

On autopilot, he drove to the ranch.

He tried his best to run, but should have known his stupid cowboy boots weren't as effective as combat boots.

Who was he kidding in trying to turn back time?

He may have once been a cowboy—hard on the outside but a soft, mushy, lovesick mess on the inside—but now, he finally understood that the past seven years had hardened him inside and out. With Jess unable to conceive, after the wedding she should probably look for a teaching job in Virginia so he could keep his job.

He trudged back to the lean-to animal shelter and saddled Fred.

Instead of doing the running himself, he climbed on his horse and rode hard until reaching the catfish pond where his wedding would be held, and where their future home was to have been built.

Before leaving, he'd have to get his deposit check from the contractor. The way things now stood, he'd prefer to put the house on hold.

He sat back in his saddle, wishing he'd grabbed his hat to shield him from the burning sun.

Insects hovered above the pond's glassy green water.

A faint musky, fishy smell rose in the heat, reminding him of past summers when he and Jessie had whiled away entire days on the pond's gentle-sloped banks. They'd stared at the clouds or each other—hadn't mattered which, just as long as they'd been together.

Now that was how it would be again.

Losing Angel was a minor setback—a good thing, since the experience had taught him he didn't have the stomach for adoption. Now that the issue was behind them, he couldn't wait to spend the rest of his life with the woman he loved.

Jessie would enjoy children through the students she taught, and Grady would continue volunteering to watch his friends' kids when needed. Otherwise, they'd enjoy each other. They'd travel and buy season tickets to every possible sport. They'd eat out every night and never have to worry about a squirmy little boy or girl hogging the bed when they'd snuck in from their room after a nightmare.

Just like that, he had a new future constructed. It wasn't the same one he'd dreamed of for literally his whole life, but that was okay. As long as he had Jessie, he didn't need a baby to be complete.

All he needed was her.

His eyes stung, but he refused to shed one more tear.

Jaw hardened, he stared out at the pond, daring his old familiar dreams to step into the light so he could crush them.

All I need is her.

"I CAN'T DO THIS." Outside of the police station the next morning, Jessie drew strength from leaning against the wall of Grady's chest. Her mother was still in the car, finishing up a call. Rose had been too upset to leave the pool house. "I can't just hand Angel to a stranger."

Grady technically held Jessie, but ever since he'd first told her the news, he'd been beyond distant. Oh, he made all the right moves, but they were somehow hollow, as if his heart was no longer in it. What did that mean? It was tough enough losing Angel. Was Jessie losing him, too?

"Grady," she asked, "how are you taking this? I didn't see you at all last night, and this morning, when Allen finally called, you hardly said a word."

"Leave it alone, Jess."

"What's that even mean? Please, Grady, don't shut me out. You've got to be hurting, too. Let's talk about it. We should—"

"Sorry." Her mother tugged on the jacket of her black business suit. She was in full mayor mode, complete with pearls and heels. "A water main burst. I had to take the call."

"It's okay," Jessie said, even though nothing could be further from the truth.

"No, this is important. I want to be here with you. Your dad texted me while I was on the call, and he'll be here in a few minutes, too. He got hung up talking to the architect for his new office." She fussed with Jessie's hair, pushing it off her shoulders. "I'm so sorry, sweetheart. I never thought this whole thing would end this way."

"Me, neither." She kissed the crown of Angel's head.

Grady didn't say a word.

The brief walk into the station felt as if she were being led to a hangman's noose.

Allen was at his usual spot behind the counter, but

upon seeing them, was also silent. He gave Grady a subtle nod, then guided them all to the break room.

Jessie held back.

She needed these last few seconds with her precious, *borrowed* Angel. "I love you," she whispered, staring into the baby's fathomless blue gaze. "How can I ever thank you for reuniting me with Grady? I guess it's only fair that now I help you reconnect with your family, huh?"

Grady said, "Come on, we need to get this over with."

"She's not a *this*. And it wouldn't kill you to open up and show some emotion. Ever since I first caught you crying out by the pool, you've acted like a robot—as though she never even mattered. But I know you loved her, too, Grady. And that's okay."

"Jess, Grady…" Allen stepped out of the break room. "I don't mean to rush you, but—"

"I'm anxious to see my granddaughter." A woman about Billy Sue's age approached Jessie, holding out her arms. Tears welled in her eyes. She wore white capris and a pretty floral top. Her dyed-blond hair looked mussed from travel. "Iris…it's really you."

She took the infant from Jessie, cradling her, then turning her back to them while sobbing.

Jessie wanted to hate the woman, but how could she? Angel had been in their lives for weeks and wasn't Jessie's to keep, yet Idabelle had lost her daughter and son-in-law. There was no comparison. No contest on the pain scale.

Jessie's heart melted, and she did the only decent thing she could, which was putting her arm around Idabelle's slight shoulders and saying, "Ma'am, I'm so sorry for your loss."

"Thank you," the older woman eventually said.

Billy Sue gave her a wad of tissues. "Are you thirsty? Would you like to sit down?" She guided Idabelle back into the break room and helped her into one of the hard plastic chairs. "This must be quite a shock. Is there anything we can do for you?"

Idabelle shook her head. "I'm sorry to break down. I thought I was strong, but ever since hearing about my daughter and son-in-law being dead, yet Iris being alive, I can't seem to stop crying. M-my daughter and I were estranged—hadn't spoken for a year. She dropped out of college when she found out she was pregnant, and we had ugly words. She took off with the baby's father—he didn't have any family. The only reason I even knew she had Iris is because Doug sent me an Easter card filled with photos." Her gaze fell to the baby. "I can't believe we fought over something so petty. So much wasted time…"

Sounded familiar. Jessie glanced across the break room at Grady. He leaned against the wall with his arms tightly folded. His expression read vacant. Clearly, he was struggling, but after meeting Idabelle, couldn't he see that returning the baby was the right thing—the *only* thing—to do?

Look at me, her heart begged. *Let me reassure you that everything's going to be okay.*

But would it be? Was losing Angel a deal breaker, and he just didn't know how to tell her?

He left the room.

"Ms. Martin," Allen said. "I've got a few papers for you to sign, and then you can take Iris and be on your way."

"Of course. Thank you."

"Do you have a car seat?" Billy Sue asked.

"Yes. I picked one up before leaving Wichita. I also grabbed bottles and premade formula, but is there a specific type she prefers?"

"We've been feeding her Enfamil," Jessie said, trying to maintain her composure, "and she seems to like it just fine. I wasn't sure how far you'd be traveling today, so I brought you three cans and plenty of bottles, liners and diapers."

"You've been so kind." Idabelle dabbed the tissues to her eyes. "In recent years, my daughter and I never got along as well as I would have liked. She took losing her father hard. I'm praying Iris and I bond the way I wish Lena and I had."

Billy Sue handed Idabelle more tissues. "Sounds like you've had more than your fair share of troubles."

"True." Idabelle fumbled with blowing her nose while holding her granddaughter. "But hasn't everybody at one time or another? I mean, from the looks of it, you all lost your entire town. I'm just so grateful for this second chance to get things right."

Me, too. Only Jessie's second chance was with Grady. Suddenly, losing Angel wasn't anywhere near as crushing as the thought of possibly losing him.

"Mom," Jessie said, "I'm going to check on Grady. Can you take care of things here?"

"Of course. Is he okay?"

Jessie nodded. After indulging in one last lingering gaze at the infant she'd always remember as her Angel, Jessie turned for the door. This brief chapter of her life may be closed, but her life with Grady had only just begun.

She should be happy about the fact, but the heaviness in her heart told a different story.

GRADY SAT ON top of a metal picnic table with his feet braced on the bench seat. The June sun beat mercilessly on the depressing concrete patio the guys occasionally used for after-hours station gatherings.

He couldn't say why he'd left the break room. His emotions were a confusing mix of resentment and sadness and regret. Honestly, Angel's presence had been too good to be true—an easy way out of the whole infertility situation that was as frustrating as it was tragic.

"There you are." Jessie exited the station through a slate-gray metal door. She'd worn her hair long and wavy—just the way he liked it—and it glinted golden in the sun. "Ritchie said you might be out here."

"I needed air."

"Idabelle will be leaving soon. Want to go inside for a last goodbye?"

He shook his head. "I said my goodbyes last night."

"Okay, well…" She pressed her hands to the table's rippled surface, tracing the lines with her fingers. "I wish you'd open up to me. Ever since we learned about Angel's grandmother, you've seemed distant."

"Sorry. I don't mean to be." He closed his eyes, leaning his head back to face the sky. Hands clamped to his forehead, he wished for the right words to come. How did he explain to Jessie that he loved her to a frightening degree? But that her infertility was an obstacle that wouldn't be easy to work past. Oh—he would. And not for one second did he look down on her or pity her. More than anything, he just felt damned sorry. By the wedding, he'd be fine. But now, he needed space.

"Then, don't." She took his hand, easing her fingers between his. "Talk to me. Tell me what you're thinking."

"Can't."

"Why?"

"Because of this." He watched her pulse quicken at the base of her throat. With his free hand, he touched her there, as if he might calm her.

"Wh-what do you mean?" Her gaze searched his.

Did he dare tell her the truth? Or would his confession hurt her to an irrevocable degree?

"Tell me. Whatever it is."

He released a long, slow exhale. "All right. With Angel at the house, your inability to have children became a nonissue. But now—"

"Don't." She dropped his hand before backing away. "I get it—which was why I told you we could never be together. All those years ago at the Dairy Barn, when I broke things off the first time, I knew."

"No, Jess. You didn't let me finish. Me struggling with the fact that it may be years before we're able to legally adopt a child—if ever—doesn't have anything to do with my love for you."

"How can you say that? It has *everything* to do with me. *I'm* the one with the problem. *I'm* the one who would be keeping you from your dreams of having your own family. Forget it, okay?" She wrenched the engagement ring he'd given her back when they'd been kids from her pinkie finger, where she'd worn it ever since he proposed for the second time. She pressed the ring into his palm, and despite the heat, the metal struck him as cold. "I release you. You are hereby free to marry the fertile woman of your dreams."

"Jess..." Tears streamed down her cheeks and he

hated that, yet again, he'd been the cause of her pain. "See? This is why I didn't want to confide in you about how I was feeling. Yeah, I'm scared about a possible future without kids, but is that really all we are to each other? Potential parents for our offspring? No. You're my best friend. The person I want to see first thing in the morning, and last before falling asleep at night. *I love you.*"

"I—I love you, too." She bowed her head. "But sometimes love isn't enough."

Chapter Seventeen

Sometimes love isn't enough.

Grady hadn't spoken a single word to Jessie since she'd returned his ring. He hadn't so much as looked in her direction. The return trip to her parents' had been beyond awkward.

Worse yet, when they got inside the house, Grady charged up the stairs and barricaded himself in his room.

Unsure what to do, Jessie sat on the foot of her bed, watching Toby munch a cricket while she worried the cuticles on her thumbs.

When Grady's door opened, and he passed by with his bulging duffel slung over his shoulder, she chased after him. "Where are you going? You can't just run away."

Only, he could.

"Would you once and for all leave me alone?" At the top of the stairs, he turned to look at her in the shadowy hall. His stone-cold stare chilled her as if it were January instead of June. "For damn near a decade, I haven't been able to let you go. I was more than willing to stand by you a lifetime, but even that wasn't enough. This infertility thing would have been our first challenge—nothing more. We could have worked through it. The next time you're lonely, Jess, I want you to remember this moment. Don't ever forget you're the one who threw me away."

"Grady, I…" *I love you. Please don't go.* But if he didn't leave now, then when? Without a baby, their breakup was inevitable.

"What? Are you going to tell me you didn't mean any of what you said at the station? And that you want to go ahead with our wedding?"

Yes! A million times, yes. But she couldn't hurt him like that. She couldn't deny him the most basic thing he'd been put on the planet to do—father a child.

He laughed, only the sound was cruel. "It's been real."

With a backward wave, he trudged down the stairs.

She wanted so badly to chase after him, begging him to stay, and she did make it to the bottom of the stairs. But then he exited out the door leading to the pool. She raced to the window to witness him enter the pool house, presumably to kiss his mother goodbye.

Poor Rose. She'd already been upset about losing Angel. Now she was losing her son.

It killed Jessie to know she was to blame, but what else could she do besides stand back and watch Grady go?

"What do you mean you're leaving?" Grady's mom asked. She'd curled onto the end of the pool house's floral love seat, resting the paperback she'd been reading on the padded arm. "Did you get called back to your base?"

"Nope. But that's where I'm headed."

"What about the wedding?"

"There isn't going to be one. Jessie called it off."

"Why?" She sat straighter.

"Great question. I think it all comes down to trust. Or a lack thereof."

She looked confused. "But, sweetheart, you two love each other like crazy. Every couple squabbles. If you'd just wait a few days instead of running off, I'm sure you'll work this out."

"Mom, I wish you were right, but there's no way."

"Where there's a will, there's always a way. Talk to her."

He sighed. "Honestly, I'm at the point where I think it would be best for me to just get back to my usual routine. You and Dad have your new house underway. You guys don't even need me anymore."

"That's where you're wrong." She took his hand, kissed his palm, then pressed it to her cheek. "I will *always* need you."

"I need you, too. And Dad. I'll stop off at the ranch before heading to the airport."

"Do you even have reservations?"

"Nope. Figure I'll play it by ear."

"Sweetheart, please tell me why you're doing this. You're usually so calm and rational. Your leaving like this doesn't even make sense."

I know. But it's the only thing I can do. "Sorry. I'll call as soon as I get back to my apartment."

She rose, and they shared a hug, and his heart broke all over again. So much loss for one day. Angel, Jessie and now his folks. The hardest part to bear was the fact that all of them were still right there. Sure, maybe the baby would be in Wichita, and everyone else back here in Rock Bluff, but the only thing truly separating them was the invisible wall of Jessie's mistrust.

THE FIRST THING Jessie did after Grady left was get her job back. Well, actually, that had been the second thing.

Her initial move had been apologizing to Rose and Ben and her parents for ever letting the wedding get so far. Though her mom had insisted it wasn't necessary, Jessie had reimbursed them for the deposits they'd put down on the cake, flowers and tent, table and chair rentals.

As long as she lived, Jessie would never forget the pained look in Rose's expression. The one that said plainer than a thousand spoken words ever could—*My son's leaving is your fault.*

Jessie didn't just accept the blame, but internalized it. She let it soak deep down inside until she hardly slept at night. But she crammed her days with activity so she wouldn't have time to think about it. She volunteered for the rebuild committee for her school. There were new books and countless classroom supplies to order. The lesson plans she'd honed over the years all needed to be redone.

When she wasn't needed at the church—where her principal and the committee met—she worked at the day care, filling in for her mom. Busy, busy, busy was the rule for her endless days.

Now, for the past hour, she'd stood at the day care's backroom utility sink, sanitizing toys. It was a thankless, tedious job and her feet and back ached.

The central air didn't adequately work all the way back here, and a fine sheen of sweat covered her forehead and upper lip. The air smelled of the rotten banana they'd found in little Jeremy Wild's cubby, and it was all she could do not to retch. Her nausea had grown worse instead of better.

"Jess?" The head teacher for the toddler room—Mandy Higgins—somehow managed to look fresh despite the heat and long day spent with rowdy kids. "Have you seen the— Oops, there it is." She took the plastic bin filled with bingo prizes from one of the shelves lining the wall opposite the sink. "How's it going? You do know you don't have to do all of these today?"

Jessie nodded.

"In fact, you don't look so hot." She pressed the back of her hand against Jessie's forehead. "No fever. So that's good."

"I'm fine," Jessie said. "Just tired."

"Then, sit down. You've still got to be reeling from Angel's grandmother showing up, and then Grady leaving."

"I'm good. I just need to finish…" Whoa. She'd stooped to grab an orange dump truck, but on her way back up the room spun.

Her vision blurred, and it became a struggle to stay on her feet.

"Jess? *Jessie!*"

Like one of the rag dolls she'd hand-washed earlier, Jessie crumpled to the floor.

"You don't look so hot, old man."

"Screw you," Grady said to Rowdy, one of the younger guys on his team. They'd been doing diving drills for the past three hours, and the canned air was killing his head. "I can't believe how out of shape I got in only a couple months."

"Yeah, yeah. Marsh told me you went and got engaged while you reverted back to being a cowpoke."

"Watch it. I'm not too old to teach you respect."

Rowdy grinned. "Wanna team up to find a couple ladies at Tipsea's tonight?"

"You know, before I left, I would have been all for

it, but now, I just wanna sleep." Tipsea's was a local SEAL hangout owned by his friend Mason's wife, Hattie. Grady used to spend damn near every night there, playing pool and searching, always searching, for the woman who might one day make him forget Jessie. His efforts hadn't worked then, and he suspected they damn sure wouldn't work now.

"Jessie? Jessie, hon, wake up."

Jessie opened her eyes to find herself on the day care's storeroom floor with her head propped on a pile of foam nap mats. "What happened?"

"You fainted." Mandy held a cold bottle of water to Jessie's parched lips. "Think you'll be okay if I leave you to call an ambulance?"

"No," Jessie said with a firm shake of her head.

"You won't be okay?" The furrow between Mandy's eyebrows deepened.

"Sorry, I meant there's no need for an ambulance. I'm fine—just overheated, hungry and probably dehydrated. Seems as though summer's coming on awfully fast."

After helping Jessie sit up, Mandy offered her the water, which Jessie took and finished off.

"Good girl," Mandy said. "Hang tight while I scrounge up something for you to eat."

Jessie breathed slow and deep, trying to regain her off-kilter sense of balance.

"Here you go." After unwrapping a granola bar and handing it to Jessie, Mandy opened a mini box of Cheerios. "It's not much, but it should give you enough energy to make it home—assuming you feel okay to drive."

"I told you I'm fine. You're sweet to worry, but I'm sure after getting cooled down, I'll be good as new."

ONLY, EVEN AFTER a week of forcing herself to eat, sleep and drink plenty of fluids, Jessie wasn't good as new, or even good as gently used.

Which was why she'd made an appointment with her doctor in Norman, and now sat in the exam room, waiting for her to come in.

"Jessie Long. Haven't seen you in ages. How'd you and your family come out of that storm?"

"We got lucky. The house and Mom's day care had only minor damage. Dad's dental office was a total write-off, but he's so excited about his new building plans that he's already feeling better."

"That's good." A tall, polished brunette, Dr. Laramie had been Jessie's physician since she'd been a teen. She knew every struggle Jessie had been through with her endometriosis, and had even been the one who'd encouraged her to at least try IVF. The doctor scrolled down her computer screen to check the vitals her nurse had just input. "Your blood pressure's a little high, and you've gained ten pounds since you were last in."

"Not sure how that's possible," Jessie complained, "when I can't seem to keep anything down."

"When you can eat, are you downing fast foods?"

"No." Jessie laughed. "All the fast-food restaurants in Rock Bluff got wiped out by the storm."

"True," the doctor said with a wry nod. "So you're nauseous, and I see in the nurse's notes that you recently fainted. Any other symptoms prior to that event?"

"I'm tired, achy, irritable, cry at every sappy commercial on TV. My breasts hurt. In general, I'm a wreck."

"Hmm…" After tapping the counter the computer screen had been mounted on, she said, "Let's do some blood work, and get a urine sample. I know considering your history that this is a long shot, but is there any chance you might be pregnant?"

Pregnant? Jessie raised her eyebrows, then clutched her belly. "I mean, I have been sexually active, but—"

"Did you use protection?"

"No." Jessie reddened. "I know that's not smart, but I really knew my partner, and since I can't conceive, I didn't think it was that big of a deal."

"Jessie, I never said you one hundred percent can't conceive. I said it's unlikely, but Mother Nature has a funny way of sometimes showing us docs who's boss."

"Okay. Well, gosh…" Afraid to even hope the doctor might be right, Jessie put her hands to her suddenly flushed cheeks. "Wouldn't that be something."

"Actually, it's not all that uncommon for couples who've been trying to conceive for years to finally find a child through adoption or surrogacy, only to then get another the old-fashioned way. Tell you what, considering your symptoms, let's do a pregnancy test first. If it's negative, we'll need to order a full battery of other tests. If it's positive—" she grinned, then winked "—I'll prescribe some prenatal vitamins and send you on your way."

The time between peeing in a cup and wandering back to the exam room seemed awkward and disjointed.

Perched on the end of the exam table, Jessie wasn't sure what to do with her hands. After all she'd been through with calling off her first engagement and the up-and-down trials of IVF, and then losing Angel and then Grady all over again, to now end up pregnant would be the ultimate irony.

"Knock, knock," Dr. Laramie said, all smiles as she pushed open the door.

Jessie's heart rate accelerated and her mouth turned desert dry. *Well?*

"There are a lot of days when I wonder why I went to med school, but today isn't one of them. Congratulations! You're expecting."

Tears welled in Jessie's eyes and joy expanded like a big pink balloon in her heart. How was this possible? How could it be this easy? After all of her worrying about never being able to conceive, she couldn't wrap her mind around the notion that her most unobtainable dream had just come true.

Would she be pressing her luck to see if getting Grady back might also be on her horizon?

FOR JESSIE, EVER since Grady left, mealtimes had been a struggle. Rose rarely smiled, Ben spent most of his days working himself half to death out at the ranch and Billy Sue and Roger worked double time to make small talk.

Typically, Jessie said as little as possibly needed in order to keep her mother happy. But on this night, everything had changed.

"What's got you so smiley?" Billy Sue asked.

"Sure wouldn't be this weather," her father said. He tossed Cotton a piece of cloverleaf roll, but the little dog was too hot to wake from his nap. The central A/C had conked out, and the repairman couldn't get to the house for two more days.

"Amen to that." Ben slathered butter on his roll.

"Well?" Billy Sue prompted. "I haven't seen your eyes

this bright since— Wait. Did you hear from Grady? Are you two back together?"

Rose pressed her hands together and beamed. "Thank you, Jesus. I knew you two were meant to one day marry."

"Should I go get my checkbook?" her father asked.

Ben said, "I'll need to give Kenny Cornell a holler— he was supposed to start brush-hogging down by the catfish pond."

"Slow down." Jessie set her fork to the plate. "Grady didn't call and our wedding's not back on—but I hope it will be, since I have news."

"Oh?" Billy Sue topped off her red wine.

All of a sudden Jessie felt awkward about having *fornicated* under her parents' roof, but even that couldn't hold back her happy tears. She took a deep breath, then blurted, "I'm pregnant!"

Her mother shrieked, then dashed around the table to squeeze her in a hug. "But I thought…"

"I know," Jessie said. "It's incredible, isn't it?"

Rose was next with a hug, then Ben and her father.

"I didn't know it was possible to be this happy," Rose said. "I can't wait to tell Grady."

"Actually," Jessie said, "if you don't mind, I'd like to tell him in person." She needed to see the relief— the jubilation—in his gorgeous blue gaze. "I've already checked flights, and if one of you will be kind enough to give me a ride to the airport, I plan on flying to Virginia first thing in the morning."

GRADY HAD JUST FINISHED scrubbing the nasty-ass frying pan Rowdy, the big slob, had left in the sink when someone knocked on the door.

No doubt Rowdy had forgotten to douse himself in cologne before leaving for Tipsea's and Wiley wouldn't turn off his truck long enough to let him use his apartment key. Marsh had recently married and moved out—lucky SOB.

The knock sounded again—this time more impatiently.

"Hold your damned horses…" Grady dried his hands on a dishrag. How the hell could Rowdy be meticulous in the field but a straight-up mess off duty? Grady hadn't realized just how sick he'd grown of sharing an apartment until he'd had a glimmer of hope for finally starting his real life.

He opened the door, and sure enough, there stood Rowdy in his straw cowboy hat, wearing a dopey grin. "Thanks, man. Wiley's being a dick and wouldn't turn off his truck to let me use his key."

"What'd you forget?" Grady asked when Rowdy rushed past to head for his room.

"My cologne!" he shouted from down the hall. "Or, as I like to call it, my *black-panther pheromones*."

Lord…

Rowdy emerged in a musky cloud that reeked. "There, that's better. As good as I smell, I should be required to wear a warning label."

Grady rolled his eyes.

"Sure you don't want to tag along, Sheikh? You can have my leftovers."

"Thanks, but I'm good," Grady said. Only, he wasn't—at all.

"Your loss. Catch you later."

For a few minutes after Wiley and Rowdy drove off, Grady stood in the open doorway, enjoying the cool twilight air. One thing he didn't miss about Oklahoma was the heat. A breeze brought with it clean, briny-scented air that did a great job of erasing his roomie's black-panther stench. That crap was more like lady repellant.

He'd just turned to head inside to finish cleaning the kitchen when a movement from the end of his complex caught his eye. A blonde's long, wavy hair caught in the breeze, reminding him of—

Jessie?

The woman struck him as lost, and he had yet to see her face. Even though he knew there was no way it could be Jessie, his pulse raced.

And then the woman glanced up and all the air rushed from his lungs.

"Grady?" Her cautious smile raised all manner of havoc in his aching chest.

Are you real?

"Sorry to pop up like this. I—I have news."

His brain couldn't seem to process her words, let alone the fact that she stood right there in blazing Technicolor on the thin strip of concrete serving as his porch.

"This area's nice. I like the palm trees. And it's wild how much cooler it is."

Call him crazy, but he wasn't in the mood for pleasantries. "Why in the hell are you here? Pretty sure we've already said all there was to say. How did you even find me?"

"Your mom gave me your address, and your dad gave me directions."

"Great. But *why*? Because you're the last person on earth I want to see." He hated taking this hard stance with her, but considering the way she'd annihilated him, did he have a choice? Right now, he was all about self-preservation, and escaping her was key. He didn't trust himself not to touch her, kiss her, get punch-drunk and stupid from the sweet strawberry scent of her hair.

"I'm sorry you feel that way." With her purse slung over her shoulder, she cupped both hands to her belly. "But I'm hoping what I have to tell you changes everything."

"Look, Jess..." Rather than look at her, he focused on a neighbor's cat that'd fallen asleep on a windowsill. "I'm sorry you made the trip out here for nothing, but whatever you're selling, I'm not buying. We're through. I can't put myself—"

"Grady, I'm pregnant." She drew her trembling lower lip into her mouth.

Had she lost her ever-loving mind?

After all they'd been through supposedly because she was incapable of ever having a baby, now she showed up on his doorstep claiming to be having his child?

"I'm serious. You know how I thought I had the flu? Well, I fainted one afternoon at the day care, and so I went to my doctor and told her my other symptoms, and she gave me the test. I know this must seem hard to believe, but—"

"Stop." He planted his hands on her slim shoulders. "I need a sec to process what you're saying. I don't mean to be cruel, but you've been through a lot. Could you have made a mistake?"

"No, Grady. I get how you'd be confused—at first, I didn't think it was possible, but it is. If I thought there was any chance of this not being true, do you think I'd even be here?"

"Okay, wow..." He raked his hands through his hair. "So I suppose now's the time when you want me to welcome you back into my heart and life as if nothing ever happened? But what if—God forbid—for some reason, you lose this baby? Then what? Are we right back where we started with you yet again pushing me away?"

"Grady, no. I swear. I love you. No matter what, I want you."

He turned his back on her to enter his apartment.

Unfortunately, she followed. "Please, believe me. This baby is a miracle, and—"

"So was Angel, and look what happened with her." He slammed the door. When Jessie jumped from the force, shame swept through him. "We're all out of miracles, Jess. You and I—we're through. I don't know what's going on with you. Maybe this is one of those—what do they call it? A hysterical pregnancy? Whatever's going on, you have to face facts—we're never going to be together."

She crumpled to his sofa as if she were a deflated blow-up toy. Hands over her face, she sobbed.

Lord, he hated hearing her cry.

"I—I really am pregnant. Why won't you believe me? The doctor said that this sometimes happens—just when couples give up all hope, or finally adopt a baby, they conceive on their own. She said it's not common, but does happen. Grady, whether you believe me or not, you're going to be a dad." She sniffed, then got up from the sofa to take a paper towel from the undercabinet dispenser. After blowing her nose, she said, "I'm sorry for the way I reacted at the police station. I was wrong, and you were right—does that make you happy?"

"No. Hell, no. What would make me happy is for you to trust me to always love you. If you're pregnant—great. But even if you aren't, this whole baby thing is a nonissue. You and me?" He pointed to his chest, then hers. "We're a team. First and foremost, it's the two of us against the world. What I want from you is more than just some baby-making vessel. I want a wife. A best friend. Someone to grow old with. It wouldn't matter if we adopted Angel or if you are by some miracle carrying our child—that kid will eventually grow up. And then we're right back where we started with the two of us. If what you feel for me isn't strong enough to sustain decades of housework and yard work and caring for horses and cattle, then there's no sense in even trying."

"You forgot some stuff." She snatched another paper towel for her nose. "What about decades of laughing, and watching movies while holding hands, and kissing..." She crept toward him, planting her hands on his chest. He froze beneath her touch—refusing to cave in to the urge to wrap his arms around her, holding on tight and never letting go. On her tiptoes, she pressed her lips to his, and he tried his damnedest to resist, but she increased the pressure and slid him a taste of her tongue. Just like that, the emotional distance between them vanished. He released his anger and fear and frustration in favor of abandoning himself to love.

He kissed her over and over, framing her dear, beautiful face with his hands. "I don't want to, but I love you. I don't know how to stop loving you."

"Then don't. Because I love you, too. Give me— *us*—a second chance."

"I think this would be more like our fifteenth stab at making things between us work."

"Who cares? I'm not keeping count."

He groaned, dipping his head to kiss her all over again. "Are you really pregnant?"

Tears shone in her eyes when she nodded.

Holy shit...

Grady couldn't define the exhilarated rush that shot through him. "One hundred percent for real? Because you know I'll still love you even if you're not."

She shot him a dirty look. "I wouldn't disrespect you like that by lying. You mean too much. I love you. I'm sorry it took so long for me to figure that out."

He dropped to his knees and slid the hem of her pretty floral shirt up. He unbuttoned her jeans, then eased down the zipper, granting himself full access to her gently rounded belly. "It doesn't look any different." He kissed a trail from the top of her pink panties to her navel. "How far along are you?"

"Don't know. I've got an ultrasound scheduled for next week."

"Cancel that appointment and make one here. I want to go with you, and there's no way I can get leave till Thanksgiving."

"How about if I keep this appointment—just to make sure the baby's healthy—then I move back here as soon as I can? My insurance money came for my car, so I need to buy a new one, then—"

"There's no way in hell you're driving cross-country pregnant by yourself."

"It's technically only half the country, and are you really going all bossy husband on me five minutes after we're reengaged?"

He shrugged before going back to kissing her tummy. "I never said anything about us tying the knot."

"You're good with us living in sin?"

"It ain't sin if it feels good." Rising, he tucked his

hands into the back pockets of her jeans, then grazed his lips up her throat.

When she closed her eyes and groaned, he knew he'd found her sweet spot.

"Although, if you don't mind giving up your fancy wedding, this weekend we could drive up to Atlantic City to do the deed."

"Do the deed?" She frowned. "You're such a romantic."

"No, honey, I'm a realist, and the reality is that the sooner we're hitched, the sooner I can move out of here, and in with you—with the added benefit of being legally tied together."

"Thought living in sin didn't matter?" She kissed him again, pressing against him, pushing her full breasts to his pecs.

"Yeah, well, maybe I changed my mind, and want to make an honest woman out of you. Marry me?"

Tearing up, she nodded.

He released her to make a quick trek to his room.

"Where are you going?" she asked.

He returned with her ring and then slipped it on her pinkie. "Don't take it off again."

"Yes, sir." She sassed him with a flirty salute.

"I'm not kidding. I'll get you a bigger ring that actually fits, but this one's special."

"You don't think I know that? Why else would I have worn it on a chain around my neck ever since the day you first left? I love you. I've always loved you, and the baby…" She glanced down, placing her hand over her stomach. "Well, the baby is just like the bow on top of my present—you're the gift inside the box. Grady Matthews, my husband, my very own cowboy SEAL."

"I like the sound of that."

"What? Cowboy SEAL?"

He shook his head, then kissed her. *"Husband."*

Epilogue

"Cotton, hush!" Jessie preferred anyone else to be answering the front door of her parents' house, but Grady, Ben and her dad were all engrossed in football, and Rose and her mom reigned over the kitchen. They'd hoped to have Thanksgiving dinner at Grady's parents' new house, but there were so many homes under construction that the contractor was behind schedule.

The smells of turkey roasting and pumpkin and apple pies baking had her mouthwatering. Jessie had offered to help with cooking, but Rose and Billy Sue shooed her out, telling her to rest. In her third trimester, Jessie would have loved nothing more, but judging by the way their son kicked, he must have a bright future in bull riding.

She tugged open the front door, only to stare. *Angel?*

Cotton barked, but then chose potential food over the excitement of company and scampered back to the kitchen.

"Hello," Idabelle Martin said. "I know this is going to sound strange, but this summer, when I took my granddaughter from you at the police station, your mother gave me her phone number and this address. She said if I ever need help, to…" Her gaze shone. "Well, I do— need help."

"Oh, okay," Jessie said. "Please, come in." The day had taken a turn for the gloomy and light sleet covered the grass and cars in a white sheen.

Angel had grown so big.

Jessie's arms ached to hold her as her grandmother passed her to come inside.

"Look at you," Idabelle said after Jessie shut the door. "You're as big as a house. When are you due?"

"January." Jessie rested her hands on her bump. "It's an awful long drive for you to come all the way here from Wichita. Why didn't you call?"

"Truthfully?" Her smile didn't reach her eyes. "Because if I called, I might not have followed through."

"With what?"

She took a deep breath, then held Angel—Iris—out to Jessie. "I want to ask you the unthinkable—to go through with your adoption plans for my granddaughter."

"But—" Holding the baby again felt familiar, yet different. In all those months apart, she'd grown into a whole new child. Yet the instant bond Jessie had felt was still there. Her love for the baby girl rushed back—only this time, with a hormonal flood of emotion. "Iris is your only family. How could you bear letting her go?"

"I can't—but I don't know what else to do. Caring for her has been wonderful, but also harder than I ever imagined. I have arthritis, and some days my hands are too weak to hold her. That scares me, you know? What would I do if there was an emergency? She needs someone young. She needs to be part of a family." She hung her head. "For that matter, so do I. Please, if you're still willing, take my granddaughter and give her a good home. All I ask is that you let me visit. I won't be a bother, and will be happy to provide financial support.

I know what I'm asking must seem nuts, but you were so upset by me taking her, I could tell how deeply you cared."

"Of course I do," Jessie said. "But this is your grand-daughter. Do you understand the gravity of what you're doing?"

Idabelle nodded. "I planned it like this—to visit on Thanksgiving. I'd hoped you'd be thankful to have my granddaughter back in your—"

"Jess?" Grady wandered in from the family room. "Oh, hey. You're Idabelle, right?" He cupped his hand to the back of Iris's head. Her curls had grown into a golden halo.

The now gray-haired woman nodded. "I see by your rings that you got married?"

"We sure did," Grady said. "Fourth of July. We had a great beach wedding—our family and friends flew in."

"Mmm, that sounds nice." Idabelle folded her arms.

"Don't mean to be rude," Grady asked, "but what brings you here—especially on Thanksgiving?"

Jessie caught him up to speed.

Billy Sue wandered in, and then Rose.

While the women chatted, Jessie gave the baby to Rose, then pulled Grady into her mother's formal living room.

"What do you think?" Her heart pounded so loud she heard it in her ears.

"Jeez…" He laughed. "Two babies? Are you sure we can manage?"

"How can we not? Think about it—we'll have a boy and a girl."

He rubbed her belly. "I don't know—this is so sudden."

"So was our baby, but you don't see me sending him away."

"Jess…"

"Don't you want this—*her*? We're talking about our Angel. She's what brought us together."

"Wrong—" He eased his hand under the curtain of her hair. "Our love brought us together. And it's going to keep us together. You need to understand this isn't like taking in a puppy. She'll be ours for a lifetime. There'll be legalities we need to tackle. Even with Idabelle's support, legally adopting Iris won't be easy."

"Since when have you ever chosen the easy path in anything you do? You're a SEAL. What you don't get is that this could be our only opportunity to have a boy and girl—a perfect matching pair of angels."

"Okay, but…" He lowered his voice. "Is this about you loving Angel, or wanting one more kid to add to our growing collection?"

"That hurts."

"I'm sorry." He brushed her cheek with his thumb. "I had to ask. It's a question you also need to ask yourself. Once we make a decision, there's no going back—at least, I hope not."

Her throat ached. "Does that mean what I think it does?"

He pressed his lips tight and groaned. "Yes. I want Angel. I never stopped wanting to make her my own—our own. I saw myself teaching her to ride her first pony and taking her to the Oklahoma City Zoo."

"Okay, then, it's settled. Ready to hash over the details with Idabelle?" Jessie's cheeks hurt from the size of her smile.

"Sure. But first—" He drew her into the sweetest

of kisses. "In case we're busy with gearing up for the newest addition to our family, I want to let you know I love you."

"Aw, sweetie, I love you, too."

They shared more tender kisses, and then Grady laced his fingers between hers as they went to officially accept their Angel.

* * * * *

*Be sure to look for the next book
in Laura Marie Altom's
COWBOY SEALS series
in December 2015!*

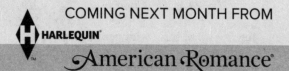

COMING NEXT MONTH FROM

HARLEQUIN

American Romance

Available July 7, 2015

#1553 THE COWBOY SEAL'S TRIPLETS
Bridesmaids Creek
by Tina Leonard
John Lopez "Squint" Mathison learned a lot in the Navy, but taming wild child Daisy Donovan requires a different set of skills. Skills he's going to need as an expectant father!

#1554 THE BULL RIDER'S SON
Reckless, Arizona
by Cathy McDavid
When newly hired bull manager and old friend Shane Westcott shows up at the Easy Money Rodeo Arena, Cassidy Beckett is forced to reveal the secret she's been keeping for six years: the identity of her son's father.

#1555 THE HEART OF A COWBOY
Blue Falls, Texas
by Trish Milburn
Natalie Todd has returned to Blue Falls with a terrible secret. She knows she must reveal the truth, but doing so will kill any feelings rancher Garrett Brody has for her...

#1556 A RANCHER OF HER OWN
The Hitching Post Hotel
by Barbara White Daille
Ranch manager and single father Pete Brannigan needs to find the right woman to make his family complete. And Jane Garland is completely unsuitable. So why can't he stop thinking about her?

SPECIAL EXCERPT FROM

H HARLEQUIN®

American **Romance**®

*Daisy Donovan has finally decided to tell
John Lopez Mathison she loves him—but first she
must convince the people of Bridesmaids Creek
she's given up her wild ways!*

Read on for a sneak preview of
THE COWBOY SEAL'S TRIPLETS,
the fourth book in **Tina Leonard**'s *heartwarming
and hilarious series* **BRIDESMAIDS CREEK**.

Jane's gaze was steady on her. "John left town last night."

Daisy blinked. "Left town?"

The older woman hesitated, then sat across from her. Cosette Lafleur—Madame Matchmaker herself—slid in next to Jane, her pink-frosted hair accentuating her all-knowing eyes.

Daisy's heart sank. "He *couldn't* have left." He hadn't said goodbye, hadn't even mentioned he was planning to make like a stiff breeze and blow away.

The women stared at her with interest.

"Did you want him to stay, Daisy?" Jane asked.

"Well—" Daisy began, not knowing how to say that she'd thought she at least rated a "goodbye," considering she'd gotten quite in the habit of enjoying a nocturnal meeting in his arms. "It would have been nice."

"Have you finally realized where your heart belongs, Daisy?" Cosette asked, and Daisy started.

"My heart?" How was it that these women always seemed to read everyone's mind? A girl had to be very careful to keep her secrets tight to her chest. "Squint and I are friends."

Cosette winked at her, and a spark of hope lit inside her that maybe Cosette wasn't horribly angry or holding a grudge with her about the whole taking-over-her-shop thing.

"We know all about those kinds of friends," Cosette said, nodding wisely.

"Still," Jane said, "it does seem rather heartless of John to leave without telling you. Had you quarreled?"

Here it came, the well-meaning BC interference of which many suffered, all secretly cherished and she'd never had the benefit of experiencing. She had to say it was rather like being under a probing yet somehow friendly microscope. "We didn't quarrel."

"But you're in love with him," Cosette said.

"That may be putting it a bit—" Her words trailed off.

"Mildly?" Jane asked.

"Lightly?" Cosette said. "You are in fact head over heels in love with him?"

Daisy felt herself blush under all the scrutiny. Sheriff Dennis McAdams slid into the booth next to her, and the ladies wasted no time filling in the sheriff, who turned his curious gaze to her.

"He left last night," the sheriff said, and Daisy wondered if John Lopez Mathison had stopped by to see every single denizen of this town to say goodbye—except for her.

Don't miss THE COWBOY SEAL'S TRIPLETS
by Tina Leonard, available July 2015
wherever Harlequin® American Romance®
books and ebooks are sold.

www.Harlequin.com

THE WORLD IS BETTER WITH

Romance

Harlequin has everything from contemporary, passionate and heartwarming to suspenseful and inspirational stories.

Whatever your mood, we have a romance just for you!

Connect with us to find your next great read, special offers and more.

f /HarlequinBooks

🐦 @HarlequinBooks

www.HarlequinBlog.com

www.Harlequin.com/Newsletters

HARLEQUIN®

A *Romance* FOR EVERY MOOD™

www.Harlequin.com

SERIESHALOAD2015